CHANCE ENCOUNTER

When her fiancé cancels their forthcoming wedding, Sophie books a holiday in Spain to overcome her disappointment. After wrongly accusing a stranger, Matt, of taking her suitcase at the airport, she is embarrassed to find he is staying at her hotel. When she discovers a mysterious package inside her suitcase, she suspects that the package is linked to him. But then she finds herself falling in love with Matt — and, after a series of mysterious encounters, she is filled with doubts . . .

SHIRLEY HEATON

CHANCE ENCOUNTER

Complete and Unabridged

LINFORD
Leicester

First published in Great Britain in 2006

First Linford Edition
published 2007

Copyright © 2006 by Shirley Heaton

British Library CIP Data

Heaton, Shirley
    Chance encounter.—Large print ed.—
Linford romance library
1. Love stories
2. Large type books
I. Title
823.9'2 [F]

ISBN 978–1–84617–794–1

Published by
F. A. Thorpe (Publishing)
Anstey, Leicestershire

Set by Words & Graphics Ltd.
Anstey, Leicestershire
Printed and bound in Great Britain by
T. J. International Ltd., Padstow, Cornwall

1

'I can't go through with it, Sophie.' His words echoed inside her head until she swayed and had to close her eyes to steady herself. But he didn't mean it, did he?

Pulling herself together she opened her lovely blue eyes and said, 'You're such a joker, Andy.' She wrapped her slim arms around his neck and kissed him soundly on the lips.

But he pulled away, his face a mask of doubts and fears. She shuddered. He did mean it, she could tell by that look. If she didn't know Andy after all the years they'd been together, nobody did. But she told herself not to panic.

Taking a deep breath, she asked, 'Is it nerves, Andy?'

'It's more than that,' he replied. He paused and averted his eyes. 'You know how much I love you,' he urged. 'I don't want us to split, but marriage is such a major commitment, a massive responsibility. It scares me, Soph. Let's give it another year or so.'

'But Andy, you made a commitment when we involved our families and made the arrangements. I know it's important to get it right, but let's face it we've been together long enough.' Her heart flipped in her chest and her stomach churned. 'You've left it late to come out with this bombshell.' Surely it was just a blip.

He shrugged his shoulders and turned away. Sophie took a deep breath and flickered her eyelids, trying to stem the tears that threatened to steal down her cheeks. And then she walked away and left him to dwell on his words. How could he say such a thing? They'd talked about the future over and over again.

But now it seemed she was on her own. After such a let-down, did she want to continue the relationship?

Her parents were furious. 'We wouldn't

want you to marry if you weren't right for each other, but it's only four days away. What about all the guests? Our Norma's already left Canada. She'll be here tomorrow. And all the money we've spent . . . '

'But, Mum, there's nothing more I can do about it. It's better than being jilted at the altar. Andy's got cold feet and that's that. End of story.' Sophie sighed deeply, giving her tense shoulders a brief shrug. Goodness knows, didn't they understand what she was going through to be rejected, especially at this late stage?

'We're not blaming you, love. But he's lucky your dad hasn't gone round there and given him what for.' It was a massive blow to be told they'd have to cancel — less than a week before the wedding day.

But that was six months ago. Looking back, she'd loved Andy with a grand passion, or so she thought. At the time she thought his words would never sink in. Now they were fading rapidly. She realised what a mistake it would have been to marry.

They'd met whilst they were still at school, and the relationship had continued simply because they were easy together, took each other for granted. But they hadn't thought it through. The decision to marry was based on expectations after such a long-term relationship.

And all she could think now was good luck to Andy. She couldn't blame him for the way he'd panicked when he realised he wasn't ready for marriage. But nor was she. What an escape!

She'd seen Andy several times since they'd parted, and although she was still very fond of him, the spark had disappeared. He was too young, too immature.

More than anything she needed her independence, she needed the space to think, to sort out her life.

It was then she decided to move into a small, but cosy flat a mile or so from her parents' place and, once settled there, her thoughts reverted to the honeymoon they'd planned, that much yearned-for trip to Barbados. But that didn't mean she couldn't get away, spend time on her own, and it certainly wouldn't be a holiday in Barbados.

The woman at the travel agents interrupted her thoughts. 'You wanted somewhere quiet, out of the way,' she confirmed.

'Yes, that's right.'

'How about Miramar? It's a lovely Spanish village in traditional style, close to the sea, but not swamped by tourists. It's completely unspoilt and there's just the one hotel. I've not stayed there personally, but I've had favourable reports. Apparently it's so peaceful. And it has a five star rating.'

Sophie dithered. She couldn't seem to make up her mind. But it did sound right for her. Undoubtedly, her mother would come up with plenty of reasons why she shouldn't go alone, just as she did when she tried to stop Sophie moving into the flat.

A snap decision was needed, and the words tumbled from her mouth. 'Why not?' She flicked her fair hair back from her pretty face and smiled. 'It sounds wonderful. Book it, please.'

'Miramar it is then.' The woman turned to the computer. 'Saturday the fourteenth, nine-thirty flight from Manchester arriving Murcia mid-day, Spanish time. How does that sound?'

'Saturday the fourteenth. That's only three days away. Great!'

Sophie left the travel agents and wandered back to the car park, hoping she'd made the right decision. But why was she suddenly full of doubts? Normally she would make a decision and stick with it. The business with Andy seemed to have sapped her of all her confidence.

★ ★ ★

It was market day and the little town of Shipton was thronging with people. She pulled out of the car park and drove

6

slowly down the main street, heading for Belmont, the village where she lived. Three days and she'd be away from all the fuss. She knew people meant well, but now she needed to get on with her life without the constant reminder of what might have been.

Once in the village she called at the newsagents for a couple of magazines. She needed to keep her mind occupied. The last thing she wanted was for time to drag. The shop was busy. It was Wednesday, lotto day, and the queue stretched to the door.

She stood patiently waiting her turn, when she felt a tap on her shoulder. She spun round. On no, not Mrs Scott. Her stomach gave a nosedive. It was just what she didn't need.

'Hello, dear,' the woman said. 'I was sorry to hear the news about you and your fiancé. How are you feeling?'

'I'm fine, Mrs Scott. But that's history now. Andy and I realised it was for the best in the end,' Sophie replied with finality.

'I know your mother was upset about it,' the woman continued, obviously wanting to dig deeper.

'We all were. It's only natural for Mum to be upset, isn't it,' Sophie replied, a smidgen of irritation in her voice. 'Both Mum and Dad wanted the best for me. And that's the way it's turned out in the end — for the best.'

The woman's face dropped. 'For the best, but . . . '

'Yes, for the best,' Sophie repeated before Mrs Scott had the chance to pontificate. The woman was decent enough, but why should she go poking her nose into Sophie's affairs. Why did people go on so? It was as though they got a kick out of looking for an adverse reaction. Some people had no tact.

To Sophie's relief, it was her turn at the counter. She paid for the magazines, gave Mrs Scott a beam of a smile and left.

Sophie was right about her mother.

'Do you think it's the right decision, darling, going on your own?' she asked, a worried frown sketching her face. 'How about Rachael, couldn't she go with you?'

'Rachael's already been on holiday, Mum. And in any case, I'm absolutely positive. It's exactly what I want.'

'Your father's offered to take a week off at the beginning of September. Why not go back to work next week and we'll all go away together, just the three of us?'

Mum was a real sweetie, but the last thing Sophie wanted was for her to fret. When would she realise her daughter was a grown woman going on twenty-four, and she could cope.

'I've booked it, Mum. Next Saturday I'll be in Miramar.' Her reply was emphatic.

She began to pack. The swimwear for the honeymoon in Barbados was rather exotic, but she'd no intention of going out and buying more. The dresses too were more than suitable. Barbados or Miramar, what difference did it make?

'We'll drop you off at the airport,' her

mother offered, still intent on fussing. But when they arrived it was so crowded that Sophie insisted she made her way to the check-in queue immediately.

Her father took the suitcase from the boot and handed it to her. 'Don't you worry about a thing, love. Enjoy it,' he said, giving her a peck of a kiss on the cheek.

It was a relief to get away. Sophie needed to collect her thoughts without being bombarded with questions, ideas, solutions, opinions — as seemed to be everyone's preoccupation since Andy had backed out of the wedding.

The queue for the check-in desk wove its way around the corner into a second hall, and it was almost half an hour before she handed over her suitcase and collected her boarding pass. But that wasn't the end of it. It was the day of a strike, and the queue for passport control was even worse.

It was almost an hour before she was through to the departure lounge.

Fortunately she hadn't long to wait there. The aircraft was on time and the passengers were soon called to the gate.

The flight was smooth and, once in Murcia, Sophie stood at the carousel waiting for her luggage. It seemed ages before the dark green suitcase appeared at the hatch and she watched it slowly coming towards her. But when she reached out to collect it, she felt another hand touching hers and gripping the handle of the suitcase.

She looked up. A tall, powerful figure of a man with a strong, dominant presence stood before her. Momentarily she was caught in his incredibly dark brown eyes and held there. Feeling foolish, she averted her gaze. And then he began to walk away — with her case.

Stunned by his action and seething through clenched teeth, she called after him, 'Hey, that's my suitcase.'

He turned and frowned at her for a moment before giving a harsh rumble of sardonic laughter. 'I don't think so,' he replied, checking the label. 'Matt

11

Williams. That's not you is it?' he asked with a challenging look and a twinkle in his eye.

'Sorry,' she said, feeling utterly deflated. Now she was making even more of a fool of herself. 'But it's exactly like mine.' She turned back to the carousel to witness her own suitcase quickly disappearing back through the hatch. What a stupid thing to do. She'd have to wait for it to re-appear now.

Eventually it came round again. Trust it to be the very last one to turn up. She collected it, wheeled it through into the outer foyer and searched for the *Village Breaks* sign. Eventually she spotted a young woman in the company uniform, and she rushed across to her, tapping her on the shoulder.

'Hello. I'm here at last. I'm Sophie Jennings,' she said, an embarrassing edge to her voice. 'I thought they'd lost my suitcase.' And then she smiled. 'I'm staying in Miramar, Hotel La Fuente,' she added, putting on her best Spanish accent, 'if that's how it's pronounced.'

'Good try, Sophie. I'm Louise. Don't worry. This is Spain — Manana. In other words, take your time. There's no rush,' she said, laughing as she ran her fingers down the list. 'That's right, you're booked in at La Fuente. The others are already here. Coach two over there,' she said, pointing to the car park. 'I'll be with you shortly.'

The coach left the airport, taking the coastal road. The first stop was twenty minutes away when two couples and a single passenger left the party. Another couple waved goodbye at the next stop, leaving eight passengers on the coach, including herself. She craned her neck to check them out.

There was a young couple sitting together, and three men and two women sitting separately. From behind she noticed a grey-haired man, and another who, judging by the style and colour of his hair, was much younger. The third had very dark wavy hair and it was difficult to tell his age. She looked again. Surely it wasn't the man at the airport, Matt whatever his name was, the one she'd accused of taking her case? That could be embarrassing.

Sophie had no idea about the women. All she knew was that one was small with dark brown curly hair, and the other seemed to be middle-aged. The couple remaining were probably on honeymoon the way they were caught up in each other's arms. Sophie felt a pang inside. But that was silly. She was over Andy now.

After another ten minute drive along the coastal road, the coach began to climb, slowly and carefully taking the hairpin bends, and passing several other vehicles on their way down. Sophie looked through the window and saw the beautiful cerulean hue of the sea glistening in the sunlight, and the rich yellow ochre of the sands.

Up above the sky was painted cobalt blue in contrast to the stark white of the village houses perched precariously on the hillsides. The scenery was breathtaking.

14

They passed through the narrow streets of the village and within minutes they came to a halt in the courtyard of what appeared to be a small hotel, also painted white and standing above the village on top of the highest hill. But the hotel wasn't as small as it appeared. Inside, the reception area was huge, the peaceful trickle of water from the fountain in its centre reflecting its relaxed atmosphere. La Fuente. That was it. The fountain.

The driver removed the suitcases from the coach to be collected by a porter who placed them on to a trolley and took them away. As soon as the keys were available, the guests were directed to their rooms and, ignoring the lift, Sophie climbed the stairs to the first floor, determined to take plenty of exercise on this holiday.

Hot and exhausted after the flight, she threw her jacket on to the bed, desperately needing something cool to wear. Lifting her suitcase on to the stand, she snapped open the fastenings and threw back the lid. With a cursory glance she made to take out the shorts and T-shirt she knew she'd placed neatly at the top.

But then her eyes opened wide and her heart began to drum noisily in her chest. Was this really her suitcase? There stuffed down the front of it was a bundle of what appeared to be papers. She gently pushed the clothes aside.

It was a large brown envelope tightly bound with a rubber band. The package certainly wasn't hers. Immediately she pushed the suitcase lid shut and stepped back. Who on earth had placed it in there?

Tentatively she flicked over the label dangling from the handle of the suitcase. It read, *Sophie Jennings*. It was hers right enough. Had the package been slotted in before they left the airport in Manchester, or when they arrived in Murcia? Could there be a link between the package and her long wait for the suitcase at the carousel?

And the dark-haired guy, Matt whatever his name was, wasn't his suitcase identical to hers? Was the package his?

Once more she opened the suitcase and stared. The package could be important. Whatever it contained could be highly confidential. It could be money or stolen documents. Her imagination was running wild. But she didn't intend looking through the package. That could start all manner of complications. The less she knew the better. It had obviously been slipped into her suitcase by mistake.

The question now was what to do next. On the one hand, if she made a fuss and contacted the police, they'd examine the papers and goodness knows what they'd find. On the other hand, why would she report it to the police if it belonged to her? And if she asked the guy, Matt if it belonged to him, and it didn't, he'd really think she'd lost her trolley.

Her decision was made. She'd go to

the reception, tell them a suspicious-looking package had turned up in her suitcase and ask them to call the police. For all she knew, it could be lethal. But was she being dramatic? Maybe she was. On a serious note, perhaps it was important to someone, and they may have reported it missing.

She left the package where it was, and locked the door to her room. As she approached the stairs, one of the men she'd travelled with came out of his room. It was the young guy with the modern hairstyle. He was probably Sophie's age and rather good-looking with lively hazel eyes.

'Hello,' he said. 'Going down to the bar?' His smile was warm.

'Hi,' she replied, adding a vibrant lift to her voice. 'I've one or two things to sort first.' She paused. 'By the way I'm Sophie Jennings.' She held out her hand.

'Justin McIntyre,' he replied and, to her amazement, he lifted her hand and kissed the back of it. 'Perhaps we'll meet up later,' he added, winking wickedly and leaving in the direction of the bar.

She smiled to herself. Quite a joker, she thought. It was going to be fun, she could tell. That's what she wanted lots of fun and lots of laughter.

Her mood had lightened already and, as she continued towards reception, she stopped herself on a whim. Her idea of asking them to call the police was foolish. She'd heard about people in foreign countries being arrested for something they hadn't done. Perhaps she should hide the package in her room and forget about it for now.

She turned and went back upstairs to her room, having decided to remove the package from her suitcase and leave it somewhere safe. But she must be careful. There was no point leaving messy fingerprints all over it, and she took a towel from the bathroom. Flicking back the lid of the suitcase, she place the towel over the package, picked it up and let it fall on to the bed, hoping it contained nothing dangerous.

Keeping the towel draped over it, she leant forward and gently fingered its contents. There appeared to be nothing but a bundle of papers inside. She was curious, but still she left it unopened.

The question now was where to hide it. It needed to be somewhere not too obvious, somewhere the maids wouldn't look when they came in to clean the room. She opened the wardrobe doors and noticed there were a couple of extra pillows and a blanket stowed on the top shelf. They wouldn't be disturbed. She certainly wouldn't need them. It was the ideal place.

She took the chair from the side of the bed and pulled it across to the wardrobe. Taking hold of the package she climbed up and pushed the pillows apart. After slipping it between them, she pressed the pillows gently back into place to make sure nothing could be seen.

With a sigh of relief she climbed back

down and returned the chair to the side of the bed. The package would be fine there for the time being, that is until she decided what her next move would be.

2

If she didn't change into something pretty cool soon, she felt sure she'd pass out. Her yellow shorts and cream T-shirt were there at the top of the suitcase exactly where she'd placed them. She pulled them out and laid them on the bed. After a quick shower, she slipped them on, combed her hair and left the room.

Downstairs at the bar she met up with Justin again. He was standing with the dark haired man who turned to face her. 'Sophie, meet Matt Williams. He's our Welsh contingent.' Justin laughed at his own comment. As she suspected, it was him, the man at the airport.

'Pleased to meet you, Sophie,' Matt said, his liquid brown eyes so intense she could almost drown in them. He focused them directly into hers and held her gaze. 'We have met before,' he said emphatically and smiled.

'That's right, Matt. Sorry about the mix-up,' she replied, feeling unaccountably annoyed she was responding warmly to his engaging smile. But that was silly. The guy had done nothing wrong, as far as she knew.

'We all make mistakes,' he insisted. 'Is it your first time in Miramar?'

'Yes. And it's lovely, too, isn't it?'

'It certainly is. This is my fourth visit. I have friends here.'

Justin was busy talking to one of the other guests who'd now put in an appearance. Sophie recognised her as one of those who'd travelled on the coach with the group. She was rather small and vivacious with dark brown curly hair.

Turning to Sophie, she smiled and said, 'You're Sophie, I believe. I'm Kerry.' She sat down on a bar stool next to her. 'This is rather different from Manchester, isn't it?' she added.

'It certainly is,' Sophie replied. 'I'm from Yorkshire, but same difference.' She laughed. 'Are you from Manchester?'

'Originally I'm from Spain. My father's Spanish and my mother's English. We moved back to Manchester when I was six.'

Matt interrupted them. 'How about drinks? What will it be?'

'Lime and lemon would be lovely, thanks.' Sophie turned to Kerry.

'And the same for me,' Kerry echoed.

Sophie soon relaxed with the little group. It was good to have met friends so quickly. They laughed together, exchanging stories, one trying to outdo the other, and it wasn't until she went back to her room that the business of the package came to the forefront of her mind again.

The more she thought about it, the more worried she became. But still, she didn't intend calling the police. Maybe she could do a little snooping. Perhaps whoever put the package in her suitcase possessed an identical one. Again Matt sprung to mind. But surely he wasn't involved?

It was going to be difficult. How could she check the colours of the suitcases when they'd be stowed away in the rooms until it was time to leave? Thinking about it, who could be a potential culprit?

Surely none of the ones she'd met so far. But she hadn't been introduced to the middle-aged woman or the older gentleman who'd travelled with the group. There was nothing for it but to remain alert and listen very carefully to what the guests had to say. That might throw more light on the matter.

Sophie changed into her bikini and collected a beach towel, leaving the room and walking down two flights of stairs to the swimming pool outside the lower ground floor. As she made for one of the sunbeds near the pool, she noticed the grey-haired man. He was sitting in a deckchair under a large umbrella. His eyes were closed and he appeared to be dozing. She was surprised to see that he wasn't as old as she'd first thought. The grey hair had thrown her. He was maybe late forties to early fifties.

She would have to wait until the next time she saw him to introduce herself. And seeing him prompted thoughts of the older woman and she checked to see if there was any sign of her in the vicinity of the pool. But she wasn't there.

After deciding where to sit, she spread her towel over the mattress and perched on the edge to apply her sun lotion. Her skin was very fair and she knew she would need to be thorough. Just as she started squeezing the bottle, she heard a call from behind her.

'Hi, Sophie!'

She looked around and saw it was Justin. He patted a sunbed beside him.

'Over here,' he said. 'Kerry's nipped back for her towel. She won't be long.'

Sophie finished smoothing on the sun lotion, picked up her towel and went across to where Justin was sitting. By that time, Kerry had arrived too.

'Good timing,' Sophie said and she sat down.

Thinking once more about the package in the wardrobe, Sophie concluded that if either Justin or Kerry were responsible for placing it in her suitcase, inadvertently or otherwise, they were playing it calm. Surely it was neither of those two.

★   ★   ★

By five o'clock, they left the pool area and Sophie returned to her room. It was difficult trying to take her mind off the package. But she made a valiant effort and tried to think instead about what she would wear that evening.

After her shower, she opened the wardrobe door to take out her trousers and matching cream blouse. Her eye caught the pillows on the top shelf as she did so. Perhaps she could take a tiny peek at the contents of the package, just to make sure there was nothing of great importance inside there.

This time she took a flimsy slip and carefully lifted down the package, placing it on the bed. A pair of gloves would have been much easier. It was a struggle keeping the slip over the package and, with shaking hands she tried to pull off the rubber band without fingering the package.

Eventually she managed it, and she carefully tipped the contents of the brown envelope on to the bed. Several pieces of paper and a smaller envelope fell out.

On closer inspection, the papers contained what appeared to be some sort of reference numbers preceded by letters of the alphabet. How very strange, she thought. What do they mean? Inside the small envelope were three photographs. The first showed a woman in a loose top and a pair of loose trousers gathered at the ankles.

Sophie recognised it as the full Asian dress, the Shalwa kamiz. The matching head covering was draped over her face and shoulders, shrouding her face completely. It would have been impossible to recognise her even if she had been a familiar figure. The woman was standing before what appeared to be a tray of something sparkling, but it was difficult to tell because there was a strong light shining on the tray, distorting its contents.

Beside her was a man dressed in a traditional western lounge suit. He had very dark hair and he could be seen partly in profile, but there was a shadow across his face, masking any clarity. The other two photographs were similar, merely different shots of the same two people, but again their faces were unclear.

What she saw puzzled her. Neither the lists nor the photographs were of any significance to her. They were a complete mystery. The package was definitely not intended for her, and she was convinced its contents were of little importance.

Someone had made a mistake and placed it in her suitcase, nothing more.

She slipped everything back into the large brown envelope, placed the rubber band around it and returned the package to the top shelf of the wardrobe.

The meal was to be served at eight o'clock, but Louise had arranged a get-together beforehand to give the holidaymakers the chance to meet each other and book any trips of interest.

When Sophie found the meeting room, she noticed the grey-haired man and the older woman sitting together chatting. She approached them and held out her hand.

'I'm Sophie.' She smiled. 'Lovely place,' she added.

The man took her hand. 'Just what the doctor ordered,' he replied. 'I'm Gordon, and this young woman,' he said with a grin, 'is Jenny.'

Jenny, a plump, homely body, turned to him. 'What a flatterer you are, Gordon,' she said with a girlish laugh. She held out her hand to Sophie. 'Please to meet you, love. The hotel is grand. I've a lovely view from my room.

But I know the area quite well. I've been to the village before.'

'You must have enjoyed it to come back again,' Sophie said and Jenny nodded.

Sophie started to move away. 'Nice meeting you both. I'll see you around,' she added and walked to the other side of the room. They seemed a nice enough couple, and Sophie realised they weren't together, but they seemed to have palled up.

Choosing an empty row of chairs, she sat down waiting for Kerry and the others to arrive. The young couple were sitting behind her, and Sophie turned and smiled but she decided not to disturb them until some time later when they were not sitting quite so close.

Louise handed out glasses of sangria and fruit juice before she started her talk. Minutes later, Kerry arrived and sat next to Sophie, but there was no sign of either Justin or Matt.

'Are the others coming?' she asked Sophie.

'I don't know. They didn't mention anything about giving it a miss, so I presume they'll turn up.'

'I see most of you have leaflets with you,' Louise said, shaking hers in the air. 'Then I'll start. First of all, domestics. The tables in the dining room are set up for fours. Would you like me to ask maitre d' to have two of them placed side by side to make a table for eight? That would mean you could all sit together. What do you think?' she asked, her face searching the group for their comments.

Sophie glanced across at the young couple. They seemed to be talking animatedly and then the young man put up his hand to speak.

'If the others agree, we'd like that.' He was obviously aware that the four singles would form a group, leaving himself and his partner to share with the older couple.

Kerry looked at Sophie. They both nodded. 'Good idea,' Sophie said. 'That way we can all get to know each other.'

She turned and smiled at the young couple.

Whilst Louise explained the arrangements for the trips, Sophie and Kerry studied the leaflet. Sophie pointed to one of the items on the sheet.

'I'd love to visit Granada. I've not been before.'

'It's really interesting. I've been there but I wouldn't mind going again.'

'Are you sure? Then we could go together. That would be lovely, Kerry. I'm not really interested in any of the other trips. We can make our own way down to the beaches on the minibus.' She paused. 'I was thinking of booking a car for a few days and touring the local areas.'

'Would you mind if I joined you?' Kerry paused and added, 'How about if we pay half each and share the driving?'

'Good idea, Kerry. I'd like that.'

'When were you thinking of booking it?'

'Maybe we should take two or three days to relax first,' Sophie suggested.

'I couldn't agree more,' came Kerry's reply.

'That's settled then.' Sophie smiled with pleasure. She was off to a good start meeting Kerry, and the others too.

The presentation over, they made their way to the dining room where they met up with Justin.

'You missed the presentation, Justin.' Sophie sat down at the table.

'I forgot all about it and then I fell asleep on the bed,' he replied. 'I had a tiring week before I left. I just couldn't keep my eyes open.'

'Don't worry. I'm sure you needed the rest, and let's face it, we are on holiday,' she chanted and gave a rebellious laugh. 'We can do as we like. There are no rules here, except our own, of course. Louise will be around in the mornings if there are any trips you're interested in.'

At that point the young couple arrived and sat down. Sophie noticed that Gordon had entered the room, too, and he was followed within minutes by Jenny.

'Hello again,' Sophie called to them.

They both smiled their recognition.

'Where's Matt?' Kerry asked, turning to Justin.

'He said he had some business to attend to. Apparently, he has friends here,' Justin told them. 'I'm sure he'll be back for the meal.'

'He mentioned about his friends when we were talking this afternoon.' Sophie's brow furrowed slightly. She wondered what his business might be. A smidgen of suspicion niggled away inside. The same question was repeating itself. Could the package be his? But he didn't seem the type to be involved in anything furtive.

The waiters were starting to serve the meal when Matt appeared in the doorway.

'Sorry I'm late,' he said, his dark eyes picking out Sophie and gazing at her intently. 'You know how it is. I got caught up in a discussion. I couldn't get away.'

'You're just in time for the soup,' Sophie said and she moved along to let him sit beside her.

'You've all had a relaxing day, I take it.' Matt's eyes remained on Sophie.

She could feel the heat surging to her face. There was something about him that sent a tingle right through her. Once more she took in his handsome good looks, his very dark wavy hair and his fathomless brown eyes. He was strikingly beautiful if that could be said of a man. And there was no doubt about it, there was some sort of chemistry between them.

But she looked away. Relationships were out as far as she was concerned. First of all, she'd lost all faith in men after the split with Andy, and secondly, she knew what they said about holiday romances.

'There's apparently a good nightclub down there on the beach. The hotel minibus goes down at nine and picks up at twelve-thirty. Anyone game?' Justin said.

'You're on.' Matt turned to him. 'I know the place. How about you two?'

36

'Why not?' Sophie nudged Kerry in a familiar way. 'What do you think?'

'I don't need to be asked twice.'

The young couple looked at each other, and it was obvious they were hoping they might be invited too.

Matt caught their look. 'Fancy coming, you guys?'

'We'd love to join you.' The young man took his partner's hand. 'I'm Chris. This is Emma, my wife.' She smiled coyly and he lifted her hand to reveal a sparkling new wedding ring.

Sophie was right. They were a honeymoon couple. 'You almost forgot yourself then, didn't you?' She chuckled. 'I suppose calling Emma your wife doesn't come easy.'

'We married last week, so it's all rather novel to us.' He looked to his wife for confirmation. Her eyes held a look of adoration for him.

Sophie turned to Kerry. 'You are here for the full two weeks, I hope.'

'Yes. I can more or less take as much time as I wish. I work for Mum and

Dad. They're really flexible. They have their own business, import/export,' she said.

'That must be interesting. What sort of things?'

'It's all non-perishable stuff — no food or anything like that. How about you?' she asked.

'I'm a medical secretary at the local hospital. I love the job. It's very interesting.'

'That's a coincidence. I'm in medical supplies. Jordan & Co. Heard of them?' Justin asked.

'I have, actually. They're our suppliers. Aren't they German-based?'

'They are. Spot on, Sophie,' he said and turned to Matt. 'How about you?'

'Civil Service,' Matt offered resignedly.

'What branch?' Justin asked him.

'White collar, desk job. Nothing exciting.'

The conversation continued after they'd retired to the bar. They discovered that Chris was in insurance and Emma was a nurse. After a sumptuous meal and excellent wine, Sophie sipped a cool, refreshing soft drink. 'That meal was delightful,' she said. 'But I feel rather porky now.'

'You certainly don't look it,' Matt replied, his eyes widening roguishly and scanning her from top to toe.

'Now stop that,' she started to say, laughing at Matt. But they were interrupted by Gordon who came in with Jenny.

'We've had a walk through the village. It's very pretty. There's a lovely church through the back streets and the views are terrific.' He turned to Jenny. 'You've been here before, haven't you, Jenny? I can see why you keep on coming back.'

'I was thinking about buying a holiday home here, but the prices are increasing by the day. And it's not something you make a snap decision about, is it?'

'No, indeed.' Gordon rubbed his hands together. 'But I like the idea of popping over here for a bit of respite now and again.'

Sophie turned to Kerry. 'We must investigate tomorrow.

'We'll do a grand tour of the village. What do you say, Kerry?'

'I'd love to.'

'I could show you around,' Matt intervened. 'I know this place like the back of my hand.'

3

It was not long after nine when they reached the playa. The beach was thrumming with life even at that time, volley ball and football both in full swing. Sophie walked ahead with Kerry, the rest of them following as they took a stroll along the promenade. The nightclub was on the opposite side of the road and they could hear the loud thumping of the beat as they approached.

This was different. Sophie hadn't been to a nightclub in yonks. She and Andy had been saving up for the wedding, and night clubbing was an unnecessary luxury for them. She dwelt on this and realised they'd missed out on the fun and excitement.

'How about a dance?'

She turned to find Matt was standing next to her. She could feel his warm breath on her neck. Swallowing hard, she felt a tiny flutter dancing in her chest at the sudden proximity of this tall figure.

The dance was a slow one. It had been some time since she'd tackled anything smoochy. But she stood close to Matt and he slid his arms around her waist and clasped his hands behind her. He pulled her close, and she could almost hear the throb of her own heart as the excitement of being with him built up inside her.

But she must be wary. She couldn't afford to become involved. As the dance came to an end, she gradually released herself from his grip.

'Enjoyed it?' Matt asked her.

She laughed in embarrassment. 'I did, actually. It's ages since I tackled a smoochy.'

'You've no man in your life, I take it,' he murmured.

Sophie shook her head.

'Then we must do it again,' he said, a glint in his eye.

It was rather impertinent of him she

thought to herself, checking whether she had any commitments or not. There was no way she was going to tell anyone about Andy. But as Matt's words sunk in, she supposed it was a harmless comment, and she must stop herself from becoming so edgy.

There was a scuffle behind them. Two of the men who'd earlier been leaning on the bar started to fight. Sophie watched in horror.

Without warning, the lights went out and there were shouts from the people in the hall. When the lights came back on the second man was nowhere to be seen. He'd disappeared like a flash. The other man, still dazed, was staggering to his feet. Matt raced across to help him.

'Are you all right, mate?' he said. 'Any damage?'

'No,' came the reply in broken English. 'But there will be damage when I get my hands on him.'

The police arrived and started to question the bar staff. After that the atmosphere was sober. The incident

had put a damper on the proceedings, and by the time the coach arrived, Sophie was weary and ready to get back to the hotel.

Letting herself quietly into the room, she slipped off her trousers and top and hung them carefully on the hanger, placing it in the wardrobe. She was too tired to take a shower at that time of night and she slipped her silk nightie over her head and slid her feet into the bed, settling down for a good night's sleep.

As she lay there motionless under a thin cotton sheet, myriad thoughts trickled through her mind, one conflicting with another. First it was the package and then it was Matt. She tried to ignore her strange mixture of feelings. She wasn't denying there was something about him that appealed to her. She couldn't put her finger on exactly what. But she must take care.

He could be the one connected with the package. He could be highly dangerous. She must be on her guard from now on. If he was involved in any sort of shady business, he was the last person she should encourage.

⋆   ⋆   ⋆

It was earlier than usual the following morning when she stepped out of bed, went into the bathroom and switched on the shower. She'd had very little sleep and she felt irritable.

Here she was hoping for a quiet holiday in this little village away from the noise and bustle of the main resorts, and things had started to go wrong from the start. But she couldn't show her frustration in front of the others. She dressed and went down for breakfast.

Everyone was down there already, except Justin. He was missing.

'He's probably nodded off,' Matt said and he pushed his chair back from the table. 'I'd better give him a knock. He was adamant he wanted to look around the village with us this morning.'

Minutes later, Matt was back. 'I can't understand it. He's not answering. Perhaps he's gone for a breath of air before breakfast.'

'I'm surprised at that,' Sophie interjected, spooning sugar into her coffee and stirring it thoughtfully. 'We're going to be walking once we leave here, unless you have other ideas, Matt.'

'Not at all,' he said. 'You're right. We'll give him another fifteen minutes and if he doesn't turn up, we'll assume he's not coming.'

But they didn't need to wait. The words had barely left his mouth when Justin came through from reception.

'We thought you'd changed your mind,' Matt said, patting the seat beside him. 'You'd better make it snappy, otherwise we'll never get away.'

'I've already eaten,' Justin told them. 'I was up at six. Couldn't sleep. I went down to the pool for a swim and then came up here for breakfast. Afterwards I went down to the little shop for a newspaper just to fill in a bit of time.'

He waved a Spanish newspaper in the air.

'But you can't read Spanish, can you?' Sophie asked.

'No, but Kerry can. I wondered if there was anything in there about the trouble at the nightclub.'

'Here let me have a look.' Kerry took the newspaper from him and scanned the front headlines. Turning to the second page she searched through the items quickly.

'Here we are. Club Rivalry. That's the heading. They're obviously referring to football clubs. There are two major teams in the province. It's usually friendly rivalry, but it sounds pretty serious for the police to have been involved. It could be down to excessive drinking I suppose — or something else.'

'All I can say is that we're lucky we're up here in the village, rather than down at the beach resort. I don't envisage any problems here.' Sophie said, crossing her fingers and hoping she hadn't spoken too soon.

They stepped outside to start their tour of the village. It was another scorching hot day and Sophie fixed her view on the horizon as it merged with the bright blue of the sea.

She smiled and turned to Matt. 'Are we ready?'

'We certainly are,' he replied, and the little group set out to explore the village.

Matt certainly knew the place inside out. It was a strenuous walk in the heat of the sun and they stopped at a little shop on the outer edge of the village and bought home-made ice cream.

The church had been renovated and when Sophie walked through its doors a peaceful aura surrounded her. The church was elaborately beautiful with gold statues and richly-carved masonry. The altar and the pulpit were bedecked with highly-scented flowers in readiness for the festival next day.

They left the church and trekked through the undergrowth towards the far edge of the village where the mountains fell steeply down into the valley below. Following the incline of the slope, they carefully scrambled down a narrow footpath and looked inside some of the caves which had been inhabited right up to the nineteen-fifties.

Some contained remains of furniture and other effects used when the caves functioned as homes for those men and their families who mined the area. Sophie was completely absorbed in the history of the village and she found the caves fascinating.

It was almost lunchtime when, hot and exhausted after their energetic walk, they returned to the hotel. Sophie decided a light lunch would be sufficient, maybe a salad and some fruit. Afterwards she decided to ring her parents and let them know she'd arrived safely.

Her mother answered the phone. 'Andy called in yesterday,' she said. 'He told us he'd been to the flat two or three times. He seemed quite upset that you'd gone away on holiday without telling him, especially when we told him you'd gone alone.'

Her mother sounded anxious. But Sophie knew what she was like. It was obvious she thought that if Andy was jealous, the two might eventually get back together. But that idea was far from Sophie's mind.

'What's it to him, Mum. I don't owe an explanation,' she replied.

Suddenly Matt came to the forefront of her mind and she started to compare the two. Andy was so young and Matt was mature and with a certain charisma that . . . She was doing it again. Daydreaming.

'Are you there, Sophie love,' her mother interjected. 'Your dad would like a word.'

Pulling herself up sharply, Sophie managed to stay with the conversation and she sighed as she replaced the receiver. Would they always regard her as their little girl?

It was time for a swim. She changed into her black and white bikini and wrapped a white chiffon sarong around her waist. That was much cooler after the morning walk. The temperature had seemed to be soaring by the minute. She opened the door of her room and stepped outside, amazed to see that Matt was there.

'Oh,' she said in surprise. 'It's you.' She was puzzled as to why he should be lingering outside her room. She felt the need to challenge him. 'Anything wrong, Matt?'

'Nothing at all, Sophie. I was just about to knock. I wanted a word with you without involving the others. I came to ask you out. I thought we might go down to the playa. There's an exclusive restaurant at the far end. How about giving the hotel a miss tonight and coming along with me?'

'I don't know how Kerry might feel.' She was stalling for time. 'I wouldn't like to leave her out.' Sophie wasn't sure she could trust herself with this man.

He looked taken aback, his dark eyes startled. 'But you barely know her. We've only been here two days. Surely she'll be fine with Justin and the others.'

Sophie gave a helpless sigh of resignation and forced herself to smile as she nodded her agreement. 'OK then. But I must have a word and tell her I won't be there tonight. It's only fair.'

His mouth creased into a smile. 'That's fine, darling. I'll pick you up at seven.'

Darling? Did he say darling? Things seemed to be advancing a little more quickly than she wanted. She must take care not to get into anything too deep. It was fine his telling her she didn't owe Kerry an explanation because they hadn't known each other for long, but he seemed to think it was fine to call her darling when they too had met only a couple of days ago.

What to wear seemed a major decision. Perhaps the powder blue dress. It was strappy and figure hugging, but so cool in the evening air. And she decided to leave her hair loose.

He was there at seven looking totally irresistible in cream trousers and a pale green shirt. Her lovely blue eyes widened and her heart started to tumble.

'You look gorgeous, Soph.' He took her arm and kissed her gently on the cheek.

She could feel her heart beginning to thump in panic. She must keep her cool and not give in to him. That was the last thing she wanted.

A taxi turned up a couple of minutes after they reached the front door of the hotel. She could feel the heat of his body as they sat in the back. To start with, silence pervaded, and then they both spoke at once. They started to laugh.

'I'm not usually tongue-tied,' Matt turned to face her. 'But I can't believe my luck escorting such a beauty.'

Sophie laughed. 'Come off it, Matt.

You could have thought of something original.' Now that the ice was broken, she felt more relaxed.

'But it's true. I mean it,' he stressed as the taxi pulled up outside Antonio's.

Inside, the restaurant was magnificent with beautiful marble floors. Several rooms were linked by arches and, from what she saw as she glanced around her, Sophie realised the patrons there were obviously well-heeled.

The menu was extensive, but mainly fish. Sophie decided on linguado which she knew to be lemon sole.

'This is absolutely delicious,' she told Matt, 'the best I've ever tasted.'

His eyes seemed to lose their dark intensity, becoming softer and more gentle. 'I thought you might be impressed, although I must say I kept my fingers crossed hoping you liked fish.'

Their eyes met across the table. He looked so relaxed. She squirmed. He was doing it again, looking at her like that. A hot flush of colour flooded her face and she took a sip of her wine.

'Do excuse me, Matt,' she said, deliberately breaking eye contact between them.

The ladies room was empty. She ran cold water into the basin and splashed her face, dabbing it lightly with one of the small towels. There, that felt better. She must try to cool it. But it was difficult.

Back at the table, the waiter came across with the dessert menu. 'I couldn't eat another thing. But I'd love coffee with cream.'

Matt smiled. 'The same for me too,' he said and the waiter disappeared.

Matt slid his hand across the table and placed it on top of hers. 'It's been a wonderful evening. I haven't enjoyed myself so much for a long time.'

'Nor me,' she said, suddenly reprimanding herself for giving such an honest, involuntary reaction. What would Andy have thought if he'd seen them together? But why should she care? She smiled inwardly. She'd been careful not to intimate anything about

Andy or the wedding. But Matt hadn't told her anything about himself.

'You asked me earlier if I had any commitments. You haven't said anything about yourself or any relationship. How about you? You could be married for all I know,' she joked.

His face was drawn into a solemn mask. He sighed. 'I was married, five years ago. But not any more.'

'I'm so sorry, Matt. I didn't mean to pry. I only mentioned it in fun. You don't have to tell me anything.'

He smiled thinly and toyed with the edge of his napkin. 'But I want to tell you. It was eight years ago when Victoria and I married. We were blissfully happy for a couple of years and then it all started to go wrong. I had to work away from home at the time. She said it was my fault she'd gone off the rails.

'She took up with one of my closest friends and when I found out, that was it. She wanted us to get back together again, said it was nothing but a fling.

But it was over for me. We divorced within the year and I've been on my own ever since.'

'It's a pity it didn't work out for you. But sometimes it's for the best to discover these things whilst you're still young.' The statement made her think about the situation with Andy and how lucky she was he'd cancelled the plans when he did, and now it had all fizzled out.

The coffee arrived, and momentarily, they sat in silence, Matt obviously thinking through what she'd said.

'I hear what you're saying, Sophie. I couldn't have stayed with her, not after knowing she'd betrayed me.'

'You said you were working away. I thought you had a desk job.'

He looked taken aback. And then he smiled. 'It was a one-off. But I was away for some time. That's when it happened.' He placed his napkin on the table. 'Are you ready, Soph? Shall we leave?'

Sophie followed him through to

reception. He was obviously known by the staff who immediately called him a taxi.

★ ★ ★

Back at the hotel, Matt asked if she'd like a nightcap. But she was tired and in truth she felt she'd been lucky not to become too involved. It was time to part.

'I'm feeling rather weary, Matt. I'd like to take a rain-check on that nightcap if you don't mind. I've had a lovely evening. Thank you so much.'

'I'll hold you to that, Soph,' he said and they walked up the stairs to the first floor and Sophie's room. 'Goodnight,' he said and she felt the closeness of his body next to hers. Her head started to spin and her blue eyes widened with alarm as he moved his hands up to hold her. He bent his head and pressed his mouth on hers so firmly that she had no chance of escape.

The kiss was fierce and charged with

fire, a kiss without end and she felt herself slowly falling. But he was a stranger. How could she allow this to happen? She eased herself away.

He brushed his thumb over her trembling lips and smiled. 'Sorry about that, but I couldn't help myself.' He squeezed her arm. 'See you tomorrow,' he added.

Her heart still pounding fit to burst, she watched him disappear down the corridor to his own room. No-one had kissed her so intimately since Andy. And she thought it would never happen again, that the spark had died. But she was very much mistaken. Not only was the spark still alive, it had blazed vigorously between them. And yet, he was a stranger, whilst Andy had been her only true love.

4

It was the day of the Granada trip. Sophie had set her alarm clock the previous night and fortunately she'd had a decent night's sleep, despite strange dreams involving Matt. She couldn't untangle the details but they weren't the sort of dreams that left her feeling upset. They were more pleasant than that.

There were few people in the dining-room when she went down for breakfast, but Kerry was there already. As far as she knew, the others hadn't booked the trip to Granada. But she was wrong. Minutes later, Gordon appeared and sat beside them.

'I thought I was the only one going,' he said. 'Jenny's been many times before and she decided to relax today. But I'm pleased to have company. It's a long journey, although I suppose I might fall asleep.' Gordon laughed. 'That's the trouble when you're my age and have to get up at the crack of dawn.'

'We'll keep you going,' Sophie said. 'That's if we're still awake,' she chuckled.

'You weren't with us last night for dinner. Other arrangements, I presume.' Gordon was fishing for information.

'That's right,' Sophie replied without revealing her whereabouts.

'Yes, she went and left me. But I'll get my own back,' Kerry promised. She turned to Sophie and, nodding her head, she put on a false yet beaming smile. Sophie retaliated by pulling a face back at Kerry. They both laughed and Gordon joined in.

After breakfast, Sophie stood up and turned to the others. 'See you back down here,' she said and she went to her room. Kerry had said it might be much cooler up there in the mountains. Sophie folded a fleecy jacket and slipped it into her backpack, just in case.

The coach was already half full and waiting outside when they left the hotel, but they managed to get two double seats so that Gordon could sit opposite.

'Have you done anything exciting so far, Gordon, or has it all been relaxation?' Sophie asked, wanting to keep him in the conversation.

'Nothing too exciting,' he replied, 'but I'm interested in jewellery. It's my trade, you know. I took Jenny, who doesn't know a thing about it, and we had a look around down at Miramar Playa and the next place on, Anna-Maria Playa. There were some lovely pieces. But I suppose that doesn't interest you,' he concluded.

'It's fascinating to look at,' Sophie offered, 'but you need pots of money to buy some of it.'

'Agreed. But there are lots of copies around these days, especially in some of the more exotic countries. I went to Turkey not very long ago, and I could have picked up watches and jewellery at half the British prices.'

'But it's not the same quality,' Kerry insisted. 'Some of it is far inferior.'

'Well, I don't suppose you want to talk about jewellery all day,' he joked and he changed the subject. 'Is this your first trip out of Miramar?'

'It's our only trip. We're thinking of hiring a car in a couple of days.'

'Snap. Jenny's agreed to share one with me. We pick it up tomorrow. It's lucky I met her actually. We're both free spirits and we get on well together. Nothing serious, of course.' He turned and looked out of the window.

The coach wound its way up the hillside and for some time they were silent. Sophie appreciated the peace and quiet. Kerry, who was sitting next to the window, had fallen asleep, and Gordon held his video camera in the air, filming the scenery through the coach window.

Something triggered off thoughts of Matt and their evening together. A delicious tingle raced through her when she thought about that kiss. But she pulled her thoughts together. It seemed rather strange that his job entailed travelling away when he'd told everyone he worked for the civil service in a desk job. But it wasn't her way to pry.

She turned her thoughts to her surroundings. The coach was slowing down now as they entered a car park. It came to a standstill and the driver announced they had arrived in Granada.

Kerry woke up with a start and rubbed her eyes. 'Sorry I fell asleep, love. You should have woken me up.'

'There was no point. You must have been tired. Don't worry about it.'

They stepped out of the coach and Sophie shivered. 'I'll tell you what, Kerry. You were right about the temperature. It's freezing.'

'Well, that's an exaggeration,' Kerry said, laughing as she slipped on her jacket. 'But it's certainly cooler.'

Sophie took the fleece from the bag and put it on. 'That's better,' she said as she zipped it up and slid her arms through the backpack. They set off climbing the hill to the Alhambra Palace, and as it came into focus Sophie's eyes were agog.

'This is absolutely stunning,' she exclaimed. 'Look at the Moorish architecture. It must have been so exotic in its time. Wasn't it the capital of the Moorish kingdom?'

'Yes. It was the capital of Granada under the Nasrid dynasty when it was a Muslim state. It's in such a prominent position high up on the mountain, it was the last Moorish stronghold in Spain. It fell to Castile in the fifteenth century.'

'Well, that's our history lesson for today,' Sophie retorted and they laughed. 'But seriously, I can see why you wanted to come back.'

After a picnic lunch provided by the tour operator, they spent time looking around the gardens. But by three o'clock they needed to be back at the coach. Shortly afterwards they were heading back to Miramar Pueblo.

'Didn't see you around, Gordon.'

Kerry leaned forward and called across the aisle of the coach.

'I got completely carried away with this,' he said, patting his video camera. 'I've plenty to show when I get back to England.' He smiled with satisfaction.

Once back in the village, the coach drew up in the hotel courtyard. Justin came to the front door to meet them.

'Enjoyed it?' he asked.

'It was wonderful,' Sophie told him. 'You should have come with us.'

'It's really not my scene,' he admitted, 'but I have been lonely,' he said and stuck out his bottom lip.

They both laughed. 'What about Matt?' Kerry asked. 'Hasn't he been here to keep you company?'

'I haven't seen him today. He must have left early.'

Sophie was puzzled. He'd been out all the previous day and now again today. He was supposed to be on holiday. Surely his business commitment here couldn't be so important.

Matt wasn't there when Sophie went

down for dinner that night and she became more and more curious. He was obviously still out with friends. But what sort of a holiday was it? He was staying at an expensive hotel and yet he had intimated he was out on business for most of the time, although they knew he had friends there too. Surely if that was the case, he could have stayed at their place. Why a hotel?

Granted, it was no concern of hers, and she knew it was finding the package that had given rise to these suspicious thoughts.

'I think Matt must have a woman hidden away somewhere,' Justin said jokingly. 'I thought he may have returned for the meal this evening, but there's no sign of him.'

Chris laughed and said, 'Joking apart, we saw him in the village this morning. You're right Justin. He did have a woman with him, rather an attractive one, too.'

Another woman? Sophie gave a caustic laugh. 'So that's his little game.'

The after-effect of his kiss last night had gradually become more intense, rather than fading as she had expected. But she certainly didn't enjoy feeling that way when there was someone else in the frame.

Kerry placed an arm around Sophie's shoulder. 'But what do we care, Soph?'

'Not a jot,' Sophie replied, and no sooner had the words left her mouth than she heard a voice behind her.

'I'm here now.' Matt had suddenly appeared on the scene.

'Speak of the devil,' Justin offered.

'How do you mean?' Matt asked. 'Have you been speaking ill of me in my absence?' he continued and he gave Sophie one of those looks meant to devastate.

But she was having none of it. She remained poker-faced.

'What a happy gathering,' he said with a sarcastic edge to his voice. 'Perhaps I'd better go out and come back in again. Start afresh.'

'Joking, old boy. Only joking,' Justin

said, slapping him on the back.

The conversation continued through-out the meal, but Sophie spoke only when it was necessary. She was seething inside. It meant nothing to her the fact that there was someone else on the scene. She and Matt were little more than strangers. It was the principle.

He'd told her he wasn't prepared to share a partnership with anyone else after that business with his wife, yet here he was giving Sophie the come-on and the next minute he was out in the village with another woman.

After the meal, she excused herself and went upstairs to her room. She started to reason things out. What right had she to judge Matt in this way? There were no strings. Maybe the woman was a friend or a relative. But each time she thought of Matt with this other woman, her stomach churned violently. She had to admit she was jealous.

At the sound of gentle tapping on the door she pulled her thoughts together.

At first she ignored it, but then it was repeated. She bounced up from the bed, stormed over to the door, took a deep breath and opened it.

Matt was standing there. 'Coming down for a drink?' he asked.

'Not tonight, Matt,' she replied, her voice lacking all emotion. 'I'm feeling rather tired.'

'Not that old excuse,' he continued. 'You're not trying to get rid of me, are you?'

'How do you mean trying to get rid of you?' She glared angrily. Again the thought of him with another woman sent her stomach into a somersault.

'Only joking. What's got into you, Soph?' he asked, a puzzled look on his face.

'Nothing whatsoever. As I said, I'm really tired.' She shook her head in exasperation.

There was a sudden glint of humour in his eyes. 'You're cross with me, aren't you? It's because I've not been around today, isn't it?' He smiled. 'Do I get the feeling you've missed me?'

'Missed you? For your information, I've been in Granada for most of the day.'

'So it's something else. Let me guess. Not there waiting when you returned?' he rasped, and now his dark eyes were beginning to show a glint of anger and frustration.

'This is a ridiculous situation. And I don't have to put up with it,' she said, her voice almost rising to a crescendo. She started to close the door.

But, with ease, he quickly pushed his shoulder against it. He reached out clasping hold of her wrists, his fingers tightening in an iron grip as he pulled her towards him. His dark eyes flashed angrily down at her. 'Oh, no you don't. Maybe you think you don't have to put up with it, but you're involved now, like it or not.'

'Involved? In what?' she asked, giving a snort of nervous laughter.

'You'll see,' he said, releasing her wrists. She stared down blindly at them

71

and they seemed still to be burning with his touch.

'I've no idea what you're talking about,' she raged. 'And in any case, I'm not interested.'

'Not interested in me, you mean?' He cupped her chin with his hand and lowered his dark head. His breath was hot against her skin. 'I think you are. You don't fool me, Soph,' he said smiling down lovingly. He lifted her chin and she knew what he was going to do.

His mouth reached out for hers and prevented any further protests. The kiss was devastating. It was then she realised the power this man had over her.

But not to give in, she pulled away and stared up at him, her incredibly blue eyes now flashing with fury. But he ignored her helpless efforts, kissed her again and stormed off down the corridor.

Whatever happened today, she was determined to ignore Matt. Who on earth did he think he was making out she was besotted by him? She made a cup of tea, climbed back into bed and thought about the situation, letting the tea go cold as she did so.

They were all there at breakfast when she walked through into the dining-room. She put on a bright and lively smile. 'Morning everybody,' she purred. 'Lovely day again,' she added and deliberately avoided eye contact with Matt.

'Coming in the pool this morning?' he asked her with a spontaneous grin.

The way he was looking at her again made her want to throw herself at him. She frowned and lowered her head, confused by her own reactions. 'I haven't decided what I'm doing yet,' she mumbled, and then she flickered her eyelashes and looked away. After breakfast she got up from the table and walked away, but she could feel him following her.

'How many times do I have to tell you? I'm not interested,' she pouted.

He reached out and placed his hand under her chin.

'Don't do that,' she shouted, but he lifted up her face and stared.

'You've got wonderful eyes. Some women would kill for them,' he said, a smile teasing the corners of his mouth.

She snatched her face away from his hand. 'And so would some men,' she replied, backing away in the direction of the pool. But she was so intent on watching what he was doing that she didn't realise her close proximity to the sunbeds.

She caught her foot on one, tripped and fell backwards straight into the pool. Down she went, water streaming into her nose and mouth. Up she came coughing and gasping. Idiot, she said to herself. When will you ever learn?

At that precise moment she felt an arm around her and she was being pulled towards the side of the pool. She looked up. It was him. How dare he? Did he think she was some child who couldn't swim and needed to be rescued? She struggled, but he held her tight.

'Cough it up,' he said, gently rubbing her back. 'You'll be fine.'

She tried to pull herself away, but it was no use. He held her firmly. And then she realised he was fully clothed. He'd jumped in to rescue her, not knowing her level of proficiency in the deep end of the pool. Better not fight him, she thought. At least he had my safety at heart.

'Thanks,' she muttered. 'It wouldn't have happened had you not followed me.'

'Excuses, excuses,' he said. He looked her up and down, making sure she was safe and then hauled himself up and climbed out of the pool. He strode off towards the building and the lower stairs.

She felt like a drowned rat. Her hair was clinging to her face and she was still suffering from the effects of falling into the water without warning. Her throat felt sore with all that coughing, and her eyes had started to sting. Maybe it was all her own fault. But now it was too late to do anything about it.

Matt had disappeared out of sight.

She picked up a towel and dried herself quickly. Now she'd have to go up to the room as she was. She needed to wash the chlorine from her face and apply moisturiser, tidy her hair and re-apply her sun lotion.

She climbed the two flights of stairs and turned the corner. There he was locking the door of his room.

'OK now?' he asked her, a complete lack of emotion on his wonderful face.

'Fine, thanks,' she said, expecting him to continue the conversation, but he carried on down the stairs and left.

She'd done it again. But despite her feelings for him, did she want someone who played the field? The answer was most definitely, no.

The others were at the poolside when she returned half an hour later. She waved and joined them.

'Changed again,' Kerry said.

'I don't enjoy sitting around in wet clothes,' she told Kerry in truth. 'I saved up to buy these. I have a weakness for swimwear.' She sat down on one of the sunbeds.

'I'll say,' Kerry said as she lay back. 'What have you done to our Matt? He seems to have disappeared. Don't tell me you've scared him off.'

'I think he has business to attend to,' Sophie offered.

'I'm surprised he spends so much time away. I think he fancies you, Soph.'

'He's not my type, Kerry.'

'What is your type?' Kerry asked with a look of curiosity on her face.

What could she say? She was floored by the question. 'I don't really know,' she confessed. 'But it's certainly not someone like Matt.'

'I don't suppose it got to you when Chris and Emma said they'd seen him with another woman, did it?'

'Well . . . '

'I can see I've touched on a sore point,' Kerry claimed. 'And yet, we don't know who the woman might have been. She could have been his sister-in-law for all we know. Anyone.'

5

Matt was back by the evening. He entered the dining-room looking dishy. He and Sophie were the only two in there. He tipped his head to one side and looked curiously at her face. She stared defiantly back at him and realised what a nice mouth he had, neatly curved and not too wide, and it shocked her when she realised she wanted to stretch over and kiss him.

'You know what I said about your eyes? The same applies to all your looks. Any woman would kill to have them,' he vouched taking in the full measure of her.

Frustrated, she gave a helpless shrug. The strap of her cream dress slid from her sun-bronzed shoulder.

'Whoosh. It's all too much,' he said and covered his face with his hands.

She started to laugh, she just

couldn't help herself, and it became infectious. Kerry and Justin arrived and, although they didn't know the source of laughter, they joined in.

'Who's game for the playa tonight? The minibus leaves at nine. Any takers?'

'Let's do it,' Justin said. 'A week's gone already and we've only been down there once. Stir yourselves, girls. Let's go.'

Kerry sat next to Sophie and they linked arms. Matt and Justin sat at the back and the young couple were left to take the middle seats. 'It's becoming a bit of a habit,' Chris said. He snuggled up to Emma. 'We've really enjoyed our holiday. You lot have made it for us, haven't they Em?'

'I'll say. We'll have happy memories when we get back home,' she murmured and then she giggled. 'We'll be going back to our new house, just the two of us. It's really exciting, isn't it, Chris.'

'We can't wait to have our own place.

It's what we've wanted for a long time and now our dream has come true.'

A touch of nostalgia swept over Sophie. That's exactly how she felt when she and Andy were planning the wedding. But what a relief it hadn't happened. She had her own flat now and she could do as she liked. She squeezed Kerry's arm. 'I'm happy as I am,' she whispered.

'Me, too,' Kerry concurred.

Soon they were down at the playa and the place was more vibrant than ever. Chris and Emma went off on their own, leaving the four of them to wander along the beach. The games were in full swing and some of the holiday-makers were still swimming despite the fading light.

'Hi, Matt,' came a call.

Sophie looked ahead. An attractive brunette stood before them.

'I rang the hotel and they told me you were on your way down in the minibus. I need a word,' she said. 'It's urgent.' She took hold of Matt's arm, led him to one side and started to whisper.

Matt looked relaxed and he nodded as she spoke to him. Finally he lifted the palm of his hand and slapped it against hers. 'See you,' he said and they parted.

Chummy or what, Sophie concluded. But if he didn't explain who she was, Sophie certainly didn't intend enquiring. But it was strange the way they confided in each other, not like lovers, but like friends, relatives even.

'Sorry about that,' he said. 'Business, nothing more.' He slipped his arm around her waist. 'Now where were we? How about calling in at a bar?'

'One of these on the beach?' she asked.

'How about the one over there?' Kerry chipped in and pointed to a quaint little place on the beach. The bar was bedecked with fairy lights and a short flight of steps led down to the bar itself.

'Looks interesting,' Justin offered, pointedly looking down the steps to see what was going on in there. 'There's music and one or two people dancing. Come on. Let's go,' he said, leading the way.

Inside, the music was loud. The place was full of twenty to thirty-year-olds, no teenagers. They were a more sophisticated bunch.

All four danced in a group. It was great fun. The music was vibrant, the atmosphere friendly and the company brilliant. She found it hard to believe she'd enjoyed herself so much.

The package. She'd not really given it a thought for the last few days. She'd promised herself she'd do some snooping. But what was the point? It was obvious none of her friends at the hotel were fretting over a lost package. She'd have noticed had that been the case. So why should she worry?

They left the dance floor and sat down. Justin ordered another round of drinks and they kept on dipping into the tapas brought to the table by the waiter.

'Anyone on the beach trip tomorrow?' Justin asked.

'We're hiring a car,' Sophie told him. 'Kerry and I.'

'Oh, I see. Sounds good,' he said a note of envy in his voice.

'What so you think, Soph? Should we invite them?' Kerry pulled a face.

Sophie's forehead creased into a frown, but she couldn't stop a smile from developing. She nodded. 'Come with us if you like,' she offered. 'We haven't decided where we're going yet, but we're leaving straight after breakfast to collect the car and then we're out for the day.'

'How about you, Matt?' Kerry piped in. 'Are you free?'

'I've nothing arranged for tomorrow. I'd love to come. How about if Justin and I share the cost? We'd prefer to pay our way.'

'Great,' Sophie said. 'It's got to be a bargain.' She laughed and looked to Matt for his reaction when she felt someone's toe touching hers. She leant back and, eyes down, she glanced under the table. But it wasn't Matt's foot, it was Justin's. Oh dear, she thought. Don't say she had two of them to contend with. But just as the thought flickered through her mind, Justin looked across at her. 'Sorry, Soph. It's my big feet again. I didn't mean to tread on yours.'

Sophie gave an inward sigh of relief and laughed. It was a pity Justin and Kerry hadn't made a go of it. They were good friends, but there was no romance. But here she was, sorting things out in her mind as though she had a definite commitment with Matt. And yet she hadn't. She was going along with him because she liked him, a lot. But she didn't intend letting him know that. And it would never end in anything serious.

The following morning, Sophie and Kerry boarded the eight-thirty minibus and set out for the playa to collect the car. It turned out to be an upgraded model with no extra charge. It was a Jeep.

They collected Justin and Matt from the hotel and Sophie drove to start. They followed the coastline to the north and came across wonderful views that almost took her breath away. She soon realised how good it was to relax and enjoy herself, rather than thinking about Matt and how he might be deceiving her, or fretting over the package that was safely stored away in her wardrobe at the hotel.

After a leisurely drive, she took a narrow winding track down to a secluded cove. The sand was pale gold and the rock pools beneath the cliffs glistened in the sunlight. There was no-one else around and they changed into their swimsuits and frolicked in the water, racing each other and challenging the incoming tide. By midday, the little group lay on the sands, recovering from their strenuous play in the sea.

Sophie turned to the others. 'I'm getting hungry,' she said. 'How about looking for something to eat?'

'I know just the place,' Matt cut in.

'It's not far from here. It's a restaurant, but they have a barbecue on the beach with a fantastic variety of fish. The sardines are especially good. Have you tried sardines?'

'I'm not really a fish person,' Kerry replied. 'Surely there'll be something else?'

'I'm sure of it, Kerry. Corn on the cob, do you like that?'

'I adore it,' she replied, licking her lips.

'I know your taste, Soph, but how about you, Justin?'

'I had sardines last time I was here. They were delicious.'

They climbed back into the Jeep. This time, Kerry drove and Justin sat in the front with her whilst Sophie and Matt lounged in the back, his arm draped casually around her shoulder.

Eventually he directed Kerry down another winding road to a beach not quite as isolated as the one they'd visited. The restaurant was a huge wooden chalet. Out at the front was a wide decking area on which a couple of chefs tended the smoking barbecue. They were already several Spanish families sitting there, some on the beach with colourful parasols protecting them and others on the decking.

The smell of fish was tempting as they approached, and they were directed by the waiter to a table close to the barbecue where they could see exactly what the chef was cooking. The waiter pushed up the parasol and handed them the menus.

Despite her best intentions not to start any sort of commitment with Matt, Sophie looked at him and wondered what it would be like being with him all the time. A deep crimson hue flooded her cheeks and when he returned her look, it was as though he knew what she was thinking. 'Something on your mind, Soph?' he murmured, a husky edge to his voice.

'Nothing important,' came her reply, but their eyes met and she detected the twinkle in his. And there was no denying he was attractive and with such an aura of vibrant appeal. She shuddered. Stop it, she told herself. If he looks again, he'll surely know what I'm thinking.

The trip ended back at the hotel where they all changed into swimsuits again and played volleyball in the pool. By this time, Sophie felt weary, not only physically, but mentally too. She had Matt on her mind and the business he had in Miramar. And who was the brunette he'd met on the beach? What was that all about? And then of course there was still the mystery of the package.

* * *

The days seemed to fly. The package was still hidden. None of its contents held any significance for Sophie and as far as she was aware, no-one had reported it missing. Had she panicked unnecessarily? She had considered telling the others, but they would probably think she was making a mountain out of a molehill. Maybe she was.

Two days before they were scheduled to go home, she was almost ready to set out for a day on the beach when she heard a knock on her bedroom door. It was Matt.

'Come in, Matt,' she said. 'I'll be ready in two ticks.' She collected her bag from the chair and turned to leave. 'I can't believe the holiday's almost through. After tomorrow, we'll be leaving for home.'

'I realise that, Soph, but that's why I'm here. It's passed really quickly, but it's been great. I'd like us to have a meal together before we part,' Matt told her. 'It's no good leaving it until tomorrow, that'll be the final night for the group. How about it?'

'I'm sure Kerry won't mind. She gets on well with Justin and the others. Did you have anywhere in mind?'

'It's a little place through the mountains where it dips down into a beautiful valley. I'd like to take you to one of the popular Spanish restaurants off the beaten track. It's a fair distance away in a little village called El Llana de Santa Barbara. It's really authentic and I think you'll love it.'

'Sounds good, Matt. What time were you thinking?'

'I thought we might leave here about seven-thirty. We'll take a leisurely run. It's probably a forty-five minute drive. As you've gathered, most Spaniards don't eat until after nine and I'd like us to be there around that time to soak in the atmosphere.'

'I'd like that, Matt,' she said, following him to the door. 'I look forward to it.'

'Me too,' he said, squeezing her hands and leaving.

Kerry was curious to know how the relationship was progressing when Sophie told her about her forthcoming evening with Matt.

'How do you mean, Kelly? I like Matt a lot and I'm sure he feels the same otherwise he wouldn't be asking me, but that's as far as it goes. In any case, we're back in England after tomorrow, so that'll be the end of it.' She hardly believed for herself that it would be over.

Her stomach gave a somersault. In truth, she knew she didn't want it to be over. She wanted it to continue. But as she'd told herself continually, it was a holiday friendship — hardly a romance.

'I think you're avoiding telling me, Soph. He fancies you like mad and I've a sneaking suspicion you feel the same.'

A rosy flush coloured Sophie's cheeks. Kerry had hit on the truth, but Sophie wasn't about to declare it to anyone.

They left the beach and returned to the hotel. Exhausted after a strenuous day, Sophie took a relaxing bath before preparing for her evening with Matt. She chose a black strappy dress with a matching stole, one of the outfits she'd chosen especially for the honeymoon in Barbados. She fastened her hair back to one side with a large pearl clip, and she left the other side draped loosely over her shoulder.

Matt was in the bar waiting for her. 'You look gorgeous Sophie. I'm surprised you've not already been swept off your feet by some man,' he whispered, trailing his fingers softly down her cheek. His touch was gentle and it sent a hot flush to her cheeks, almost setting her skin on fire.

Sophie stiffened. He had touched upon something she wanted to forget. She had almost been swept away by Matt, but not quite. And she'd pushed all thoughts of him to the back of her mind.

They set out for the village of El Llana de Santa Barbara, and sat in comfortable silence for several minutes before Matt started to point out several sights during the journey. They passed through villages and tiny hamlets before they began to climb into the mountains. It was quiet and peaceful.

'I'll miss all this,' she told him. 'It's

back to the hospital next week.'

'You're not looking forward to that, I take it.'

'I love my work. I've worked there since I left college. It's great to be amongst all those caring people. But the time here has flown. I'd love to stay another week. It's been such good fun.'

'But doesn't it make all the difference getting up in a morning and leaving for a job you enjoy.' Matt took her hand and squeezed it. 'I always feel sorry for people who have boring jobs, reluctantly having to push themselves day after day.'

'I couldn't agree more. I meet lots of lovely people at the hospital. Some of the patients have serious illnesses, but it's amazing how they manage to stay jolly and optimistic.' She turned to him. 'I take it you enjoy your job,' she said.

'Very much so. It certainly keeps me on my toes,' he said and pointed ahead. 'Here we are. This is Santa Barbara. What do you think?'

The sun had disappeared and it was

getting dark as they drove down to a small village in the valley below. It was in the form of a bowl completely surrounded by mountains.

'It's really picturesque, Matt. I love those Moorish-styled houses on the hillsides. And look over there,' she said pointing to a huge white building in the distance.

'That's it, Soph. That's the restaurant.'

The village street was almost deserted and the huge building, dimly lit in the fading light, became more prominent.

'It gets quite cold here in the winter,' Matt told her, 'especially when the sun is low in the sky.'

'I would imagine it's hot in the summer, sheltered by all these mountains.'

'Exactly,' Matt replied. 'And you'll feel the heat when we get out of the car, despite the time of day.'

The restaurant stood back from the tiny street, and they drove to the car park at the rear of the building.

Matt took her hand and they walked round to the front through the gardens which were interspersed with patio areas.

They entered a large vestibule and were welcomed by the maitre d' who showed them to a table near a window.

'What a magnificent view of the mountains. They look so majestic.' Sophie's eyes lit up. 'It's a lovely little village.'

'That's exactly why I brought you here. I wanted you to remember Spain in all its rustic glory.'

'I'll certainly remember this,' Sophie said, keeping her gaze on the wonderful vista.

Matt stretched his hand across the table and placed it over hers. 'I hope we can keep in touch when we get back to England.' His eyes looked deeply into hers as if searching for something. 'I wanted to tell you I've enjoyed the holiday immensely, and I have you to thank for that.'

The look sent her senses spiralling

out of control. She stared back, mesmerised by those dark, mysterious eyes. And then she took a deep breath.

This was neither the time nor place to show her true colours. She must try to remain calm. How long had she known him? Less than a couple of weeks. If he wanted to keep in touch that was fine by her, but she must let the relationship develop gradually.

'Yes, I've enjoyed it too. But everything has to come to an end at some time,' she said, thinking about her relationship with Andy and the way it turned out. 'Just a few more days and I'll be back at work again,' she said, trying to steer the conversation in a different direction.

Matt was quiet for some time. And then he looked across at her. 'I wanted you to know I'll not be travelling back with the group.' His eyes were still firmly focused on hers. 'I have to stay here for a few more days.'

'Oh, I see.' Sophie didn't see, but she wasn't about to ask him why he should be staying in Miramar when surely his job in the civil service called him back. Was his decision to stay connected to his relationship with the women he'd met on the beach?

'I don't think you do, darling,' he said. 'Unfortunately, that's as much as I can say at the moment.'

Her feelings of warmth seemed to disperse. Now he was being secretive. How did he mean that was all he could tell her? It was all a mystery. Although she wouldn't dream of trying to persuade him to tell her why he was staying, she couldn't help feeling needled that she didn't know the reason.

But, despite her underlying doubts, she enjoyed the rest of the evening, Matt made sure of that. He kept the conversation going and there was no time to dwell on anything else.

It was late when they returned to Miramar and La Fuente. The others had retired for the night and the bar was empty. Matt held her hand and they walked along the corridor together towards her room. She placed the key in the lock and swung open the door.

'Thanks for a lovely evening, Matt. It's been wonderful, a treat to finish off the holiday.'

'It's not finished yet, my darling,' he said. 'We've all the fun of tomorrow to come with the gang.'

'That's if you're available.' The words slipped out. Sophie could have bitten off her tongue. She entered the room and Matt followed.

'How do you mean?'

'It's just that you've been taken up so much down at the playa, I wondered if you might be down there again tomorrow,' she stuttered, tilting her face towards him.

He looked down at her with such deep emotion in his dark eyes that her heart suddenly began a rapid tattoo. She stared back with dazed eyes, and before she knew it his mouth closed firmly over hers. Fire danced in her lips and she wondered whether the heat had

98

come from him or from somewhere deep inside her.

Slowly he released her. 'If I didn't know better, I'd say you were jealous,' he said, his firm gaze focused on her lovely blue eyes.

But those eyes flashed with irritation as she gazed up at him. How dare he suggest she was jealous? She was nothing of the sort. She was merely suggesting he may not be available.

'Matt. I'm neither jealous nor annoyed. We've had a wonderful holiday fling, and that's the end of it as far as I'm concerned,' she snapped tersely.

He glared back at her and then his mouth took on a lop-sided grin. 'Only joking, my love, but surely it was more than a fling?' he said, giving her a peck on the cheek. Without waiting for an answer, he added, 'See you tomorrow,' and left.

It seemed she'd put her foot in it again. He was obviously annoyed with her, the way he'd glared back. And why did she have to spoil it? It seemed every man and his dog were being made to answer for Andy's rejection of her. That was firmly tucked away in the past now. She'd not even thought about Andy during the holiday.

But she must try to remove that chip from her shoulder. She must change her attitude and her expectations. If she continued to suspect all men of playing with her emotions and eventually casting her aside, she'd never trust anyone.

She decided she'd make it up to Matt the following day. By then she would have calmed down. But, despite his assurances, it was still a mystery as to why he was staying on in Miramar.

6

It seemed that Matt was keeping his distance the following day. The four of them lazed around the hotel pool, poked fun at one another in the lightest possible way, and played volleyball in the water. Sophie watched pensively as Matt gazed towards the mountains. He was not a happy man.

'Anything wrong, Matt?' she asked.

'Nothing I can't handle, Soph,' he replied, barely reacting to her comment and keeping his eyes firmly fixed on the mountains. He lifted himself from the sunbed. 'I must go. I'll see you tonight.'

But Sophie didn't see him that evening. Had he been available she would have made an effort to sort out any misunderstandings, and apologise for being so terse. But he didn't appear.

Disappointed, she left the bar and went up to her room. Things had come to a close and now she must pack. She placed her suitcase on the bed and started to collect her things from the wardrobe. It was eleven o'clock now and she must have her suitcase packed and ready for collection the following morning.

If Matt didn't turn up then chances were she'd never see him again. They had neither exchanged addresses nor telephone numbers. How stupid and stubborn she had been. How could she have let things get the better of her?

Once everything was neatly packed in her suitcase, she lifted it down from the bed and wheeled it towards the door. That was it. The end of her holiday. But what a marvellous holiday it had been.

She couldn't have wished for better company. She'd made a lifelong friend in Kerry, Justin had made her laugh and Matt — what could she say?

She pulled her thoughts together and opened the wardrobe for the final time to make sure there was nothing left in there. She glanced casually towards the top shelf and noticed that the pillows appeared to have been disturbed.

The package. It suddenly came to her mind. She had clean forgotten about it. Each day she had kept on checking that it was still there, but now it looked as though someone had rifled between the pillows.

She pulled the chair to the front of the wardrobe and climbed up, carefully easing the pillows apart. There was no sign of the package. She lifted the blanket down from the shelf and then the pillows one by one. The shelf was empty. The package was missing.

Someone had been into her room and taken it. Her stomach began to churn again. What was going on? She was becoming paranoid.

It took a massive effort for her to calm down and think rationally. Struggling to pull herself together, she ignored her strange sense of deep apprehension. It was obvious the owner of the package had now retrieved it, rightly or wrongly, realising his earlier mistake.

That surely let Sophie off the hook. She needn't worry about it any more. It was no longer her problem, her responsibility. Out of sight, out of mind.

Kerry knocked on Sophie's door early the next morning. 'Sorry if I woke you, Soph, but I have to leave early. Mum rang late last night to tell me Dad's not well. She booked me on an earlier flight home. Here's my address. Keep in touch, love.'

'You've taken me unawares, Kerry,' Sophie replied, stifling a yawn. 'I'm sorry about your Dad. I hope he pulls round. I was looking forward to travelling back together. But we can meet up back in England. My address and phone number,' she added, scribbling them quickly on a scrap of paper. 'Hope you can read it.'

Kerry gave her a hug. 'I'll ring you.'

That was the first disappointment, Kerry leaving so early. Surely Matt would be there to see them off at eleven. But he didn't turn up.

That was fickle of him making such

an issue of telling her how much he thought about her, but not even turning up to say goodbye.

Justin fooled about and managed to take her mind off the fact that Matt hadn't appeared on the scene. They reached the airport and checked in.

'Nice to have met you, Sophie.' It was Gordon who approached her.

'Same here,' she replied, 'and you too, Jenny. You never know, we may meet again in Miramar. It's a lovely place and I know you've been several times. I'd certainly love to go back there.'

'Sophie love, I'm sure you would. Do take care.'

Justin gave Sophie a smacking kiss and said, 'If it hadn't been for that Matt guy beating me to the draw, I'd have gone for you myself,' he added, grinning from ear to ear.

'I know,' she said, rolling her eyes and flickering her eyelashes playfully, 'I'm in great demand.' She laughed.

'Seriously though, Soph. What's happened to Matt? We've seen nothing of him. And he didn't turn up to wave us off.'

'I can't imagine where he is, Justin. I'm as much in the dark as you are.' She was about to continue when she heard a call.

'Soph, Justin.'

She turned. It was Matt. 'Glad I caught up with you. Sorry I missed you at the hotel. I so wanted to say goodbye to you both.' He took Justin's hand, shook it vigorously and gave him a bear hug. Turning to Sophie he said, 'I hope you didn't think I'd forgotten you.'

Justin, being diplomatic, moved away.

'Sorry we have to part like this. But things became complicated,' he said, his strained, tense body holding her close. 'I'll be in touch. Promise.'

'Don't worry, Matt,' she said, relieved he'd at least managed to get there. She slipped her arms around his neck and clung to him fiercely. 'Thanks for everything.'

He took her face in his and possessed

her lips in a long, lingering kiss. Her heart sang.

Gradually he let go. 'Where's Kerry?' he asked.

'She left early. Her father wasn't well. Her mother booked her on an earlier flight. She said to say bye to everyone.'

'That must have been disappointing for you, Soph. You were best buddies.'

'We were. But we'll keep in touch.'

'I must go, Soph. Remember what I said. I promise I'll ring you.' He took her by the elbows, pulled her towards him and gave her a final kiss. He turned to Justin who had wandered away during the little interlude and called out, 'See you around.'

'You bet,' came Justin's reply as he drifted back towards Sophie. 'I'm about to board my flight now,' he told her. 'I'd normally take the Manchester flight but I'm going via Gatwick. There's a company seminar on security tomorrow. It's in London and I have to be there. Take care, love. I'll miss you,' he concluded kissing her on both cheeks and waving as he moved towards the gate.

Reluctantly Sophie boarded her flight to Manchester. Would she ever see Matt again or was it an empty promise he'd made?

Chris and Emma were on the same flight as Sophie and they chatted all the way to Manchester. Emma was excited about their new house and, although Chris didn't show the same enthusiasm, Sophie knew he was equally excited.

Once at Manchester Airport, Mum and Dad were there to meet her. 'Enjoyed it?' they asked in unison, looking at each other and laughing.

'And how. It's been brilliant. I just feel on a bit of a downer coming home.'

'Oh, don't bother about us,' her father said, laughing again.

'You know what I mean, Dad,' she said, realising her comment had been rather tactless.

'I know you've enjoyed it, love. I can tell by the look on your face,' he said.

'And we're delighted, aren't we, Linda?'

'I was so worried when you said you were going alone,' Linda confessed. 'But I needn't have bothered. You look wonderfully refreshed.'

Sophie settled in the back of the car and they left the airport in the direction of Belmont. 'But, honestly Mum, it is good to be back. I have missed you, really I have,' she added in all sincerity.

'We know that, love,' she replied. 'It'll be busy through the village. It's the motorcycle rally this weekend, the one organised for charity and there's a lot of camaraderie what with the crowds of people there and the interest in the bikes.'

They reached the hill leading to the village, but there was so much traffic about, they had to take it at snail's pace. When they reached the brow Sophie spotted Andy inspecting one of the bikes with a couple of friends. Not wishing to draw attention to him, she said nothing.

'There's Andy,' her mother pointed

out. She waved. 'He's been to the house umpteen times, asking when you'd be back.'

Sophie waved her hand. 'As I said before, Mum. It's over. I've grown up since that little episode.'

But was it the end of it? Sophie had been at her parents' house no more than half-an-hour when there was a knock on the door. It was Andy.

'Sophie, you're back at last,' he said, giving a loud sigh and holding out his arms towards her. 'I called at the flat but I guessed you'd still be here with your mum and dad. Enjoyed it did you?'

'It was a wonderful holiday, Andy,' she said, giving him a peck on the cheek and then backing away in the hope he would realise she had no intention of resuming the relationship. She looked at him. He was sweet and he was innocent. He was as attractive a guy as any woman might want, but she knew now he wasn't for her. Parting had been traumatic, but she'd pulled through relatively unscathed.

'What are you doing this weekend, Soph? There's a trip out to Brockleston with the motorbike lot. The lads are going and some of the girls, too. Do you fancy it?'

'Sorry, Andy. I've already made arrangements for the weekend.' She'd decided to spend some time with her Mum and Dad. They'd been so understanding despite their occasional comments about Andy. She wanted to take them out on Saturday evening for a meal at the local Italian restaurant.

'Don't reject me, Soph. We still have a lot going for us. We've been together all this time. Surely that means something.'

'Believe me, it does, Andy. I'll always love you as a friend, but I'm not in love with you any more. We need to get on with our own lives now.'

His face dropped. 'I'm sorry about what happened. You've no idea how much I regret it. Can't we start again?'

'Sorry, Andy.'

He turned and opened the door to leave. 'I'll never stop loving you, Soph. And I'll never give up on you.'

Sophie went back into the lounge. Her mother was sitting on the edge of the seat. 'Well?' she said.

'Well, what, Mum?'

'Have you made any arrangements?'

'Yes, I have as a matter of fact. I've telephoned La Ronde and we're all going out for an Italian meal tonight, just you, Dad and me.'

'What about Andy?'

'I keep telling you. We're through, it finished, it's over,' she stressed.

'Well, we can't tell you what to do. But the lad made a mistake and now he regrets it, I know that.'

'But I don't regret it. And you're right, Mum. You can't tell me what to do. I need to make my own way now.' Sophie turned and went upstairs. As if she hadn't enough to contend with, Andy pressuring her, now there was Mum too. But she'd cope, that was for certain.

★ ★ ★

Sophie found the evening at La Ronde relaxing. It turned out to be good fun and just what she needed to take her mind off other things. She told her parents about the holiday, about the friends she'd met and the places she'd been. But she intimated nothing about her friendship with Matt whilst she was in Miramar, despite the fact that she'd not stopped thinking about him since her return to England.

She knew she must be careful. Mum was wise to lots of things, although on this occasion she didn't suspect a thing. Sophie didn't mention the package either. She knew if she even touched on the subject, it would worry them. That was the last thing she wanted.

When she left for work on Monday, she felt a little apprehensive. The holiday had been great, much better than she'd ever dreamt it would be, but that was it, back at work until the Christmas holiday. That was the trouble with holidays. They could be unsettling. But when she arrived and met up with her colleagues, she felt a strong urge to become involved again.

Mr Prothero the consultant radiologist welcomed her back. 'We've missed you Sophie,' he told her. 'There have been so many mistakes in the reports, it's just not true.'

'There you are, then,' she joked. 'At least you recognise a good thing when you sample it.'

'I recognise a bit of cheek when I sample it,' he replied and joined in the laughter. 'Right, Sophie. Let's get started. There's so much to do. We've had a nasty spate of chest problems, probably viral, and the workload has almost doubled. We've had whole groups of people here for X-rays. Unfortunately I haven't had much success with the temporary girl. She doesn't seem to grasp the terminology.'

'Some of them haven't had the training, Mr Prothero. But we're short-staffed, especially it being summer break time. Mrs Charlton does the best she can. She accepts anyone well qualified and with good keyboard skills. The terminology's another thing. Some of the new staff pick it up reasonably quickly and I'm sure with experience they'll get a grasp of it.'

'Well let's hope you're not away again for some time. I don't want to go through that again.'

'I'll try not to slip off on some exotic holiday, sir,' Sophie said, tugging an imaginary forelock, 'but I can't promise.'

She turned off the lights in the X-ray consultation room and switched on a small lamp to throw light directly on to her notepad. She picked up her pencil and started to take down the notes Mr Prothero dictated as he studied each x-ray. He was of the old school of consultants. He disliked dictating his notes on to a machine. He much preferred Sophie to sit with him and take down the reports in shorthand.

Many of the secretaries hadn't used

that skill for some considerable time, and when they had to write down unfamiliar medical words or phrases at speed, they often couldn't cope. But Sophie enjoyed being there at the coal-face so to speak. It was far more interesting than processing the reports from a cassette machine.

Once she became engrossed in the task, all other thoughts slipped her mind. It was important that she listened carefully and transcribed the notes accurately.

She knew she would have a huge workload after being away from the hospital for three weeks, and Mr Prothero's reports were only a part of that workload.

At eleven o'clock after completing some of them, she was called to the side room of the operating theatre where consultant gynaecologist Mr Richards asked her to collect the patients' records and take down notes on the surgery he'd carried out.

By lunchtime she was exhausted and

she felt as though she'd been back at work for ever.

'I've been run off my feet this morning,' she said to Val, one of the older secretaries. 'I've only been back three-and-a-half hours. They certainly get their pound of flesh.'

Val laughed. 'Wait until you've been here as long as I have, you'll learn to pace yourself.' She folded the newspaper she'd been reading. 'Fancy a stroll through the grounds, get a breath of fresh air and walk off our lunch?'

'Good idea, Val. I've eaten so much during the last two weeks, I'll be a stone heavier if I don't watch it.'

'How did the holiday go?' Val asked.

'It was wonderful,' she enthused. 'I met some really nice people there.'

'Anyone special?' Val enquired.

Sophie blushed. 'Yes, there was. His name was Matt. He was a real nice guy but something of a mystery. I never really found out what his job was, and he didn't travel back with us which I found rather strange. Come to think of it he said he'd give me a ring but he never asked me for my phone number.' Her heart sank. She hadn't thought about that since she returned. That was it. She'd never hear from him again.

'Did he give it to anyone else?'

'Not that I know of. In any case the only person I could contact is Kerry, and I'm sure she won't be seeing him again to give him my number.'

'That's unfortunate. I take it you were besotted.'

'Not besotted but we seemed to gel as soon as we met. I liked him a lot, but I didn't tell him that.'

'Did he tell you?'

'Yes, I suppose he did.'

'What was wrong in your telling him you liked him?'

'I think you know, Val. Once bitten and so on.'

'But surely if it was nothing too serious, you could have given him a hint, a clue if you like. You can't spend the rest of your life being cagey just because you've been let down in the past.'

'I suppose I could have told him, but for some reason I tend to hold back these days.'

Val laughed. 'I know it's not funny but I'm thinking about Mother. She'd call it a good 'fault' not to be too forward, and I suppose she was right in a way, but not to the exclusion of leaving someone you care for without contact numbers.'

'I'm afraid that's how it happened. It was such a rushed parting, we over-looked it. I suppose I should have been a little more pro-active.' Sophie sighed. It was fine telling herself all this now, but she knew she wouldn't have been forthcoming. She certainly wouldn't have asked him for his telephone number. As an afterthought, she added, 'Guess who called on me the moment I arrived home?'

'Not Andy,' Val replied, shaking her head. 'You must be joking.'

'He says he wants to start afresh, but

I told him it's out of the question. We're finished.'

'I don't know how he has the nerve.'

'I only hope it doesn't continue. I need some peace in my life. I need to settle down again after what's happened.'

They were back at the front door of the hospital. Sophie walked inside and turned to Val. 'I suppose I'd better get down to some more work.'

'Me too,' Val said. 'Sorry if I've sounded the agony aunt. Do as you think fit Sophie. It's just my way, giving advice. I've had a lot of experience myself,' she said, a wistful note in her voice.

'I know you mean well,' Sophie replied, conscious of the fact that Val had recently been through a very sad bereavement. 'I'll see you later on,' she added and she set off down the west wing to her office.

The afternoon was equally as hectic as the morning. Sophie didn't complete all the notes but there was always tomorrow. At least the first day back was over.

It had been a struggle coping with all the work but she'd put in a good stint and hoped to complete the backlog by the end of the week.

It being her first day back at work, she'd promised her parents she'd eat with them, but then she must get back to the flat and hopefully have another early night. She'd had so many late nights in Miramar, she had a lot of catching up to do.

When she thought about Miramar it triggered off memories of her friends there, and she was forced to admit to herself she did feel rather lonely. Perhaps after the evening meal when she'd returned to the flat she'd telephone Kerry, ask how her father was, and maybe suggest meeting up.

Mum kept her longer than she'd planned and it was almost nine o'clock when she returned to the flat. She picked up the telephone and dialled Kerry's number.

It rang for some time and just as she was about to replace the receiver, a voice answered. It was a man with a foreign accent. Surely it couldn't be Kerry's father. She'd said he was ill?

'Is Kerry there please?'

'Who is speaking?' His reply was abrupt.

'It's Sophie. We met in Miramar.'

'I'll get her for you.'

Sophie could hear his voice in the background calling for Kerry. He sounded extremely brusque.

'Hi, Sophie. Back down to earth with a bump?' Kerry cried.

'And how! You can say that again. I've had one busy day, believe me. I was ringing to ask how your father is. But was it your father who answered the phone?'

'Yes, it was. He's much better now. Thanks for asking.'

'The other reason I called was to ask if you'd like to come and stay for the weekend. We could go out for a meal and maybe take in a club. Have you much on?'

'I can't this weekend but how about next week?'

'I'd love that, Kerry. I'm really looking forward to seeing you again. By the way you don't happen to know Matt's phone number do you?'

'Sorry I don't. Did he not give it to you?'

'He intended to, but in the rush of things he must have forgotten. But there's nothing I can do about it now. I don't even have Justin's number to ask him.'

'Nor do I. In my rush to catch the early plane, the only number I got was yours. That's really unfortunate, Sophie. I knew how much you liked Matt.'

'Don't worry, Sophie replied, trying to keep her voice as light as possible. 'It's not all that important.'

She'd tried the last avenue. If Kerry didn't have the phone number, and neither of them had any means of contacting Justin, that was the end of that.

'How about if I come over Friday evening? Is that too soon? I could come on the train from Manchester.'

'That would be super. I'll tell you what, I'll meet you at the station.'

'Sounds great, Sophie. I'm really looking forward to meeting up again.'

7

Andy was persistent. During the next two weeks, he called at the flat three times. It was becoming a nuisance fobbing him off each time, but he refused to listen, despite Sophie's pleas.

'Andy, please understand. We're through. Our relationship could never be the same again. We can still be friends, but nothing more. I've already made a fresh start by moving into the flat. You need to start afresh too. Go out, enjoy yourself. We've both missed out. All the time we were saving we stayed in, we never went anywhere, when you think about it, we were too young to be so restricted.'

Sophie hoped that finally Andy would realise she meant what she'd said. Surely she'd been emphatic enough. He was the one who'd triggered the whole thing off, made the first move. And she still maintained that, as it turned out, it was the right move for her.

He left the flat, his handsome face concealed by a heavy frown. Sophie watched him walk down the path, shoulders slumped. She felt sorry for him. But that was no basis for reconciling the relationship and, for her part, the past couldn't be reversed. When he'd called off the wedding, he'd made a decision that affected the two of them. Now he would have to live with it.

There was a mountain of work at the hospital the following day. There had been a serious road accident involving a bus and a lorry. A large majority of the passengers needed to be x-rayed and Sophie was called in by Mr Prothero to process the reports as a matter of urgency.

It was late when she returned from work and pushed open the door. An envelope on the doormat caught her eye and she picked it up. She didn't recognise the handwriting. It was postmarked London. She was puzzled. She didn't know anyone in London.

She turned the envelope over to see if there was a return address on the back. It was blank. But why was she messing about? The quickest way to find out who it was from was to open it.

She slipped her thumb inside the flap and tore the envelope open, drawing out a single page letter. As she unfolded the sheet of paper her stomach churned. It was one of those letters anyone dreads receiving. The words were clipped from the newspapers. They read:

For your own safety forget about the package. It wasn't for you. Disclose the details to anyone and you'll suffer the consequences.

She stared at the sheet in her hand, a jumble of thoughts scurrying through her mind. Another dilemma. Should she go to the police? The message said she mustn't disclose the details, and if she did, maybe whoever had sent the note would carry out their threats. She turned and locked the door, her legs becoming weak as she considered the consequences.

She was scared. It didn't make sense. How had they managed to get hold of her address? Unless, of course, it was taken from her suitcase on her return journey.

She sat down in an armchair and toyed with a multitude of thoughts. If she didn't contact the police, she'd be forever wary, on her guard, suspicious. Perhaps that was the best way forward after all.

She lifted the receiver and dialled the local police. 'I need to speak to someone in confidence,' she said. 'I can't explain over the phone, but I've had a threatening letter. I don't know what to do. But I don't want a uniformed officer calling at the house. I'm scared to come down there in case anyone sees me.'

The officer took down her details. 'I'll send someone round, love, but you've not given us much to go on and we are busy just now. But someone will come. Leave it with me.'

Sleep didn't come easily that night. And when she did fall asleep, every little noise seemed to rouse her again. It was eight o'clock when she glanced at the clock in the bedroom. If she didn't get a move on she'd be late for work.

It was Friday and Sophie's mind was focused on Kerry's visit that evening. It was fine and sunny and she hoped it would stay that way. They would go out for a Chinese meal at the Red Sun that evening. It was too much of a rush for her to meet Kerry from the train straight after work and then prepare a meal.

Over the next couple of days she'd planned to take Kerry into the Yorkshire Dales and show her some of the famous landmarks.

The train was on time. Kerry appeared in the distance. 'Hi, Soph,' she called, as she stepped off the train, arms outstretched. 'Lovely to see you. It seems ages since we were in Miramar.'

'I know,' Sophie replied, giving Kerry a hug. 'You look great. You haven't lost your tan.'

'I take after Dad. With my complexion it's easy,' she said and laughed. 'But you have fair skin, Soph. You can't expect to get a dark tan with skin as pale as yours. Anyway I love that golden bronze look.'

'Then we're both happy.' Sophie flashed a smile and took the hold-all from Kerry's hand. 'Let me take this. My car's just outside. The flat is only ten minutes away.'

Once at the car, Sophie slipped the bag on to the back seat and they set out for home. Most of the rush-hour traffic had cleared by the time they reached Shipton, and they had a straight run up the hill to Belmont. She parked the car on the roadside and Kerry followed her into the flat.

'We're eating out tonight. I thought it might be rather a rush preparing a meal. Is that OK?' Sophie asked her.

'Fine. It'll give us plenty of time to catch up on the latest gossip.'

'This is your room,' Sophie said, placing the hold-all on the bed. 'I've booked the table for seven-thirty. The bathroom's through here if you'd like to freshen up.'

'I'll be ready in ten minutes,' Kerry said, picking up her vanity case and going through into the bathroom.

As she did so, there was a knock on the door. Sophie called out, 'Who is it?' hoping it wouldn't be Andy paying another visit.

'Police, love,' was the reply.

That was inconvenient, but she couldn't grumble. At least someone had turned up. She slid off the chain guard and opened the door. The officer was in plain clothes and he held out his card.

'Constable Charlton, love. Now, how can I help? I understand you've had something through the post.'

'Come in,' she said. 'I have a friend here at the moment and we're almost ready to go out, but I'll put you in the picture and give you the letter.'

Sophie explained about the package she'd found, and her decision not to report it whilst she was in Spain. 'I thought it was irrelevant,' she told him. 'I must say I thought it strange when it disappeared. But I was ready to come home by that time. So I thought no more about it.'

'What was in the package?'

'Just a few slips of paper with numbers on them and a couple of photographs. As I say, they didn't mean anything to me.' Sophie described the photographs to the officer.

'Let me take this back with me,' he said carefully slipping a plastic bag over the paper. 'Has anyone else touched this?' he asked.

'No, just me.'

'I'll make some enquiries. Whatever you do, don't open the door without checking who's there. There's no reason for anyone to suspect who I am, so don't worry. I'll be in touch.' The officer left the flat and Sophie felt a sense of relief that she'd been able to share her fears.

She went into her bedroom and slipped off her suit. 'Are you out of the bathroom, Kerry?' she called.

'I've just finished. I'll be ready in a couple of minutes.'

Time was passing and Sophie needed to freshen herself and change into something more casual. She chose her jeans and a sweater.

'There I'm ready too,' she said.

She locked the door to the flat and took out the car key. As she was climbing into the car, she heard a voice behind her. She turned. It was Andy.

'It hasn't taken you long to get involved.'

'What on earth are you talking about? I'm not involved with anyone. And if I were it would be no business of yours Andy.' She closed the car door and started the engine. Who on earth he was referring to, she hadn't a clue. He knew nothing of her movements in

Miramar, so he couldn't be referring to Matt.

She set off for the Red Sun and saw through her mirror that Andy was sitting in his car. She hoped he wasn't about to follow her. But as she turned the corner, he was still there.

'He sounded bitter,' Kerry observed.

'It's a long story. We were going to be married but he got cold feet at the last minute. As it turned out, I realised I didn't want to marry him anyway. But now he seems obsessed with clinging on to me. I've simply no idea who he was referring to.'

'Could it have been the man who visited you this evening?'

'Oh, I didn't know you'd seen him.'

'I didn't. I heard the voice though.'

'Well, I doubt Andy was referring to him. That's another story in itself.' She drew up at the traffic lights and turned to Kerry. 'Having said that, maybe Andy was watching and he got hold of the wrong end of the stick. He obviously thought the policeman was a boyfriend.'

'Policeman? I didn't realise it was a policeman. Nothing wrong is there?'

'Not really. I'll tell you about it some time. But tonight we're going to enjoy ourselves. No more talk of Andy or the police.'

They both agreed the Chinese meal was delightful and it was late when they returned. To Sophie's relief, there was no sign of Andy. On the Saturday they went to Otley and looked around the market, later driving on to Grassingham for a long walk in the countryside.

On Sunday, they took a leisurely stroll across the moors at Belmont and stopped at The White House for lunch. It was half past two before they were back at the flat and Kerry went into her room to pack. She had a train to catch at three thirty.

'It's been good fun, Soph. We must do it again. I'd ask you across to our place, but we're on the outskirts of Manchester. It wouldn't be the same, unless of course you fancied a day's shopping in Manchester.'

'I'd love that. I've had no retail therapy since I shopped for the wedding.' She laughed. 'But that's history now.'

'You're certainly determined to forget it and get on with your life, Soph. I admire you for that. It can't have been easy.'

'You're right. It wasn't at first, but now I'm completely independent and raring to go.'

'I'll have a word with Mum when I get home and find out when's convenient for her. Unlike you, I can't just make the decision. We have to fit things around the business. You do understand, don't you?'

'Of course I do. That would be lovely.'

Once at the station, Kerry climbed aboard the train and waved goodbye to Sophie. The weekend had been great, a resounding success. Time had passed so quickly that Sophie hadn't thought about the package or the letter until she was driving back home. Her stomach churned. She'd no idea what the police might make of it but all she could do was leave the matter in their hands and hope there were no come-backs.

A couple of days later Kerry telephoned to thank Sophie for the weekend. 'By the way, I've mentioned your coming over here to Mum and she thinks the best time would be the weekend of the twenty-fifth. If you take the train I could meet you at the station and bring you over here. Can you make it?'

'I don't need to look in my diary, Kerry. I'm certain I'll be free, seeing that I'm not booked up with romantic assignations,' she said, tossing back her hair and laughing.

'I know what you mean. But brilliant you can manage it. Give me a call when you've booked your ticket. I could collect you any time of the day. As you know we're flexible at this end. If you could travel on the Friday, it would be an added bonus.'

'I'll try my best. Thanks for the call.

I'll be in touch.' With that she replaced the receiver and turned to finish off her ironing. Mum had offered to do that for her, but Sophie felt the need to be completely independent. Once her mother started to become involved, there was no knowing where it would end.

She'd be calling round and doing the cleaning and the washing, asking Sophie round for meals and before she knew where she was, she'd be trying to persuade her to go back and live at home. And that wasn't an option for Sophie.

It seemed Sophie's word to Andy had done the trick. She didn't see him again. But she did see PC Charlton. He called to tell Sophie they might have a lead.

They had checked the fingerprints but they needed to eliminate Sophie's before they could proceed. 'I'd like to call with a colleague tomorrow and we'll take your prints here at the flat. Is that OK?' he asked.

'It's fine if it's going to help.' She smiled. 'My prints won't go on record, I hope,' she joked.

'They'll be destroyed at soon as we've checked them, love,' P.C. Charlton told her. 'Don't worry about that.'

On his second visit he brought along his sergeant who told her they were pursuing a lead but he could reveal nothing more.

'It would be best if you told no-one of this,' he stressed.

'I've told no-one, not even my parents,' she said.

'The thing is, sometimes culprits get wind of what's happening and go to ground. We'd like everything to progress as normal.'

'I understand,' Sophie told him. 'I'll not mention it to anyone.'

Kerry was at the station to collect her. Sophie hadn't been to Manchester for over a year and she was looking forward to the two of them spending time wandering around the shops.

Kerry's house was maybe fifteen

minutes' drive out of the city and her mother was there to meet them. Sophie gasped to herself as she entered the mansion. She'd not expected anything so majestic. The business must be doing really well if they could afford to live in a place like this.

'Nice meeting you, Sophie. I've heard a lot about you. Kerry tells me you had a lovely time in Spain. She has told you her father is from the Valencia region hasn't she? We love it out there.'

'You didn't want to stay and live out there, then?' Sophie asked.

'It was the business. We couldn't do that. This is our base,' she said, turning to Kerry. 'Show Sophie to her room, love and then we'll have a cup of tea.'

'We don't want to be too long, Mum. I have a surprise for Sophie. But I shan't tell her what it is, not until we arrive.'

'Arrive? Where are we going?'

'You'll see,' Kerry added, a beam of a smile lighting her face.

'I can't wait. Judging by the look on

your face, it's going to be something good.'

'Trust Kerry to be secretive. She's been like that since she was a toddler,' her mother said, pointing to her daughter and laughing.

'Don't give all my secrets away, Mum.'

For Sophie, the excitement built and after Mrs Fernandez offered a second cup of tea, she could wait no longer.

'Thanks, but I don't think I could drink another drop, and I can't wait to know what the surprise is.'

'Come along then. Let's go. Leave your case upstairs until we come back.'

They climbed into the car and set off to a little place called Inglethorpe which was completely unfamiliar to Sophie. She racked her brain but she just couldn't think what on earth the surprise could be. Eventually they came to a row of cottages in a pretty village. Kerry pulled up outside one of them and took hold of Sophie's arm.

'Come along,' she said. 'We're here.'

Kerry slipped her arm through Sophie's and rang the bell. She turned to Sophie, opened her eyes wide and nodded her head. 'This is it.'

After a few seconds, the door opened. Justin was standing there, a huge grin on his face. He held out his arms. 'Sophie. It's been all of six weeks since I saw you,' he said and hugged her close. He turned to Kerry. 'Hi there, Kerry. It was a stroke of good luck we met. Come in you two.'

'It's wonderful seeing you again, Justin,' Sophie said, her face aglow with elation. She turned to Kerry and then a tiny frown started to develop. 'But I thought you hadn't seen Justin.'

'I hadn't, not until last week. I was in Mason's the jewellers when we came face to face. I couldn't believe my eyes and, if I'm right Justin, nor could you.'

'I couldn't.'

'A jeweller's shop. Don't tell me you were looking for an engagement ring or something like that,' Sophie bantered.

'You must be joking,' he replied. 'No,

I was looking around, nothing more.'

'How did things go in London? Interesting seminars?'

'Very. They were mainly about the misuse of drugs and how easily some of the hard drugs could get into the wrong hands. But the security's really tightened up now.'

'But you don't handle the drugs, Justin. How could it apply to you?'

'The seminars were aimed at all staff, not just those handling the drugs.' He rubbed his hands together. 'Anyway, what have you been up to since I last saw you? Seen anything of Matt?'

'I was about to ask you that. You remember we met in the airport at Murcia. He said he'd give me his telephone number, and take mine, but in our haste, we both forgot.'

'Don't worry, Soph. I have his number and his address.' He took out a slip of paper from his wallet. 'Here take that and copy it, but give me it back.'

Sophie's heart tumbled in her chest.

Now she was able to contact Matt. She took the paper and studied it. Although she knew Matt was originally from the north, it seemed he was now based in London.

8

What a stroke of luck meeting up with Justin and getting hold of Matt's address and telephone number. Sophie decided it would be best if she phoned him from home. She didn't want to show her eagerness by ringing whilst she was staying with Kerry.

They stayed with Justin for an hour or so and then Kerry stood up to go. 'We need to get back now. Sophie hasn't even unpacked her case yet. You mentioned going out for a meal together tomorrow night. How about the bistro we passed on the way here?'

'Good Taste, was that it?'

'It was something like that.'

'Well spotted Kerry. The food there is great. Eight o'clock do you think? I'll book it,' he said without waiting for an answer.

The arrangements made, Kerry and

Sophie left Justin's place and travelled back. 'I'll give you time to sort your things out. Mum's made a meal for us. I thought afterwards we might take in a club, if you feel up to it.'

'Sounds great, Kerry. I'll leave it until after the meal to change. But I wouldn't mind a quick shower first.'

'You have an en suite, Soph. Feel free. Be down by seven if you can manage it.'

Sophie opened her bag, took out the clothes she'd brought and hung them in the wardrobe before taking a shower. Afterwards she slipped on a pair of cropped trousers and a T-shirt. There'd be time to decide what she was wearing after the meal. In any case, she didn't have much choice having brought the minimum. There was no point carrying a heavy bag when she was travelling by train.

The meal was delicious. 'I don't know whether I'm up to going to a club,' Sophie said, holding her stomach and laughing. 'I can hardly move after all that food. It was lovely Mrs Fernandez. Thank you. Now that I'm in a place of my own, I don't get food like that any more, not unless I go to Mum's for a meal.'

'We mums do get it right sometimes, but it's a pleasure, love,' Mrs Fernandez offered as she started to clear the table.

'Right, Soph. Let's go up and get ready. We'll leave about nine.'

Sophie decided to wear her white trousers and a black top. She'd tie up her hair and leave it wispy, giving it that wild look that was all the fashion. She opened the door of the wardrobe and went to take out the trousers when she noticed something that looked familiar.

She edged the clothes already in there along the rail and there it was. The Shalwa kamiz, the one she'd seen on the photographs. If it wasn't the exact one, it was certainly identical.

Her stomach began to somersault. Why was such a garment hanging in the wardrobe in Kerry's house? These garments were worn by Muslim women.

She was puzzled. Maybe Asian dress was one of their lines for export, or more likely import for the Muslim community in England. That would be it. But what was it doing in the wardrobe here?

Sophie slid the clothes back to the end of the rail and hid the garment. Could Kerry be connected with the business of the package? How much did she know and, even more to the point, had Kerry stolen it from her room? If she had, then she knew Sophie had called in the police. But then why should she leave the garment there in the wardrobe? Could it be to scare her?

It seemed she could be playing with fire. She just couldn't believe the business of the package had anything to do with Kerry. And it probably hadn't. This was obviously a coincidence. She must act as though she knew nothing about the garment. But she needed to be wary. If she let slip that the police were investigating, then she could be in danger.

Once ready Sophie went downstairs. 'Do I pass?' she asked, putting on a show, twirling and flicking her hands dramatically in the air.

'If you don't, I've no chance,' Kerry replied, looking her up and down and nodding vigorously. 'You look great.'

It was imperative Sophie kept up the banter and remained lively. The last thing she wanted was for Kerry to suspect she knew about the garment. Each time the business of the package came to mind, she felt a niggling feeling in her stomach, but she tried to cast all thoughts of it aside and concentrate on other things.

Sophie found it difficult to concentrate on the music at the club, but she kept up the act and it was a relief when they left. At one-thirty in the morning, they tiptoed into the house, trying to stifle their giggles. The last thing they wanted was to wake anyone at that hour.

'See you in the morning,' Kerry whispered. 'But not too early.'

Sophie opened the door to her room and closed it quietly behind her. She drew the curtains and switched on the light. The wardrobe door was slightly open, the way she'd left it.

She popped her clothes on a hanger and slipped it inside, checking to make sure she had seen the Shalwa kamiz in there and that it wasn't a figment of her imagination. It was still there. She closed the wardrobe doors and slid into bed. Did she tell P.C. Charlton about this when she returned to Belmont, or did she ignore it?

She slept fitfully that night, trying to weigh up in her mind who could be the owner of the package, and contemplating the note she'd received from somewhere in London.

And then the thought struck her. Hadn't Justin been in London round about the time she received the note. And not only that, Matt was based in London.

By the time she went down for breakfast next morning she felt more shattered than ever. It was wearing her down thinking about the package and its contents, the Shalwa kamiz in the wardrobe and now her thoughts about London. Perhaps a day's shopping in Manchester city centre would help to take her mind off things.

Fortunately Kerry was in a good mood. She'd obviously had plenty of sleep, and she buoyed Sophie up, chatting to her, making suggestions about the fashions they saw and generally being lively. This helped Sophie take her mind off the problems and when they returned it was so late they had little time to prepare for the meal out with Justin.

They managed to arrive at Good Taste with minutes to spare. Justin was already there and he was his usual jokey self. By the time they'd finished entrée, they were well into vying with each other with stories of amusing incidents. There was no doubt about it, Justin was a likeable personality, and Sophie could in no way suspect that he had any connection with the package. Nor Kerry for that matter, but there was the evidence in the wardrobe back at the house.

On the way back, Sophie thought about the events of the weekend. The highlight had most certainly been their evening out with Justin. It had been great fun, reminiscent of the times in Miramar. This triggered off thoughts of Matt and their closeness.

She couldn't wait to return to Belmont and telephone him in London. London — that was the place where the note had been posted. She wished she hadn't channelled her thoughts in that direction.

There was a strange car outside the house when they returned at ten fifteen.

'I don't know who that can be,' Kerry said. 'I don't recognise the car.' She opened the front door and Sophie followed her in. There were raised voices coming from the lounge. They stood there and listened. The clipped tones of a man with a foreign accent

152

boomed out, 'You're wrong!'

'That's Dad. He's having an argument with someone. I've no idea what it's all about.' Kerry whispered. 'Wait there. I'll pop my head round the door and see what's happening.'

Sophie stood back whilst Kerry opened the door and took a peek. And then she stepped inside the room.

'Matt,' Sophie heard her saying. 'What on earth are you doing here?' She turned to Sophie and started to back out of the room. But Sophie had heard her say it was Matt, but did she mean her Matt, well not exactly her Matt, Matt Williams she meant? She stepped forward, pushed past Sophie and entered the room.

Two men were standing in front of the door hands behind their backs. Matt was facing Mr and Mrs Fernandez. Sophie assumed it was Mr Fernandez for she hadn't met him until now. His face had an irate glow, whilst Mrs Fernandez was pale and she looked troubled.

It was as though they were being confronted by Matt. What was he doing here anyway? Kerry had said she didn't know his address or telephone number, and yet here he was.

Matt glanced across and his eyes, usually black, velvety and intense, met Sophie's. But there was no warmth in them. If looks could kill, she'd be extinct.

'I'd like you to leave us, Sophie. I have business to conduct and I need to speak in confidence,' he demanded, his angry eyes now raking her. 'You stay, Kerry.'

Why did he wish to speak to Kerry and not her? What was this charade?

But determined not to be involved, Sophie backed out of the room and went upstairs to her bedroom. If this business was something between the two of them, her mother and father included of course, then it wasn't for Sophie to intrude.

She took off the clothes she was wearing and changed into her casual trousers and T-shirt, placing the hanger back in the wardrobe. She brushed the other clothes to one side and it was then she noticed the Shalwa kamiz had disappeared. A shiver went down her spine as she flicked the clothes backwards and forwards to check again. It was definitely missing. The panic returned.

She flopped down on the bed, her head spinning now. She'd become embroiled in something very sinister but she'd no idea what it was. How did Matt fit into the picture? Was he in it with them, a party to it, whatever their business was? He'd given her nothing but a cursory glance with those cold eyes.

She lay back and rested her head on the pillow. All she wanted now was to get back home to Belmont. She didn't want to be involved in anything that might provoke danger. She would prefer having to fend off Andy time and time again rather than having to cope with anything like this.

She was startled when she heard the front door bang loudly. She sat up abruptly wondering what was happening. Then she heard a light tapping sound on the door of her bedroom. She froze to the spot, somehow unable to move. Another knock followed, slightly louder this time. She swallowed hard and dragged herself up, slipping her foot out of the bed and on to the floor.

'Who is it?' she called.

'It's Matt. I need to talk. Please open the door.'

'It's open,' she muttered, turning her head away. If he thought he could come to her room reverting to his nice guy image after the way he'd reacted downstairs, he could think again.

He entered the room and held out his arms. 'Sorry about that,' he said. 'You must be wondering what on earth's happened.' He paused. 'Grab your things. Let's go. I'll explain in the car.'

Explain in the car! He'd do nothing of the sort. If he thought now that Kerry was out of the way, he could treat her like some bimbo, he could think again.

'And where do you intend taking me?' she ground through clenched teeth.

'Don't ask any more questions until we get to the car. Just pick up your bag.' His voice was brusque.

'But where's Kerry,' she added scathingly. 'She's going to wonder why I've left.'

'Kerry's not here.'

'So it seems,' Sophie said, a light, ironic lilt to her voice.

Matt took hold of her arm and with a little pressure he steered her towards the door. The house was empty as they left but Kerry's car was still outside. They walked to the end of the road where another car was parked.

'Get in,' he ordered. 'I didn't want to leave you there alone. We'll sort out somewhere for you to stay until we've ironed out this little business.'

'Sort out somewhere for me to stay? How do you mean?' she asked, her voice almost reaching a crescendo. 'I have somewhere to stay. All I need to do is take the train back to Shipton. I don't need any help, thank you very much.'

'You've no choice. I need you here until we find out one way or another what's happening. We need to sift through the evidence.'

'The evidence? For what?'

'You're asking too many questions. That's as much as I can tell you.'

'I just don't understand any more.'

'Don't try to, not yet.'

'What happens now?' She folded her arms and gave him a look meant to slay him dead.

'Why the look? And what's with the twenty questions? I've explained as much as I can.' He stepped closer and took hold of her arm but the movement was intimidating, overpowering.

Defiantly she stood her ground, resisting the natural urge to back away. 'Now that you've stopped bossing me, perhaps you'll let go of my arm,' she snapped.

He glared, stunned by her response. 'Don't mess me about, Soph. This is serious,' he rasped.

'Then treat me with a little more courtesy,' she snorted, sticking her nose in the air and walking ahead of him.

He started to laugh. 'Now come back here, and let's start again,' he begged, his tone implacable.

She stopped and turned once more. What could she do? She was captivated by the man. She could barely take her eyes from him. But, not wanting him to guess what she was thinking, she dragged her eyes away. And all she could hear behind her was a deep gurgle. He wasn't just laughing, he was laughing at her.

That was it. How dare he laugh? 'Just because you're a man, doesn't give you the right to laugh,' she said waspishly.

He slicked his hand through his hair in a manner she recognised as irritation. 'OK then, Soph. I can only give you a brief outline. I'm with the police. We've taken the Fernandez family in for questioning but we haven't enough to charge them with as yet, and that's why I need to get back to the station pronto. We know about the package. I was the one who took it from the wardrobe. But I didn't put it into your suitcase. Someone else did, and that's what we need to find out. Sorry I couldn't let on. We also know about the note you were sent. Nasty business that. Your locals have brought us up to date.'

'The police? I see, a white-collar desk job, that's what you told us. You've been deceiving us all this time, Matt, checking up on us.'

She followed him into the station, aware he was simmering in silence. Perhaps she'd gone too far. After all he was trying to solve this crime, whatever it was. And maybe she was needed to provide evidence of the package and the note.

But all this time she'd been thinking of no-one but herself. That was selfish. What about Kerry? What did Matt mean when he said he'd taken the

Fernandez family in for questioning? Did that include Kerry? If that were the case, the implication was that she'd been involved all along. Surely not.

Time dragged. A female officer made Sophie a cup of tea. 'Now we need to take you to a safe haven as soon as you've drunk your tea, love.'

'Why do I need a safe haven?' she protested.

'We need to keep you out of the way, just until we've solved this one. There are obviously others involved. Inspector Williams insists you're not to be let out of sight until he gives the command.'

'He does, does he? We'll see about that.' Sophie collected her backpack and set off towards the door.

'Sorry, Miss Jennings, no can do. I told you his instructions. For your own good you must abide by them.' Two officers standing nearby took her arms and led her back to the female officer.

9

Sophie didn't see Matt again that night, nor did she see Kerry or her parents. What on earth had they done? She knew there was some connection with the papers and the photographs, but what?

A police car drew up outside the station and Sophie was led to it and asked to sit in the back. The female officer sat next to her. There was no use protesting any more. She couldn't fight them. She must do as they said.

They drew up at a house on the outskirts of the city. Sophie didn't recognise the district, but the area was gloomy and the house was drab.

'Come along, Sophie,' the officer said, taking her by the elbow and steering her towards the front door of the property. Once inside, the officer lit the gas fire and they sat down in two shabby armchairs.

'I'm P. C. Leaventhorpe, but call me Joanne. I know you must be wondering what's going on, but I can't tell you any more than you already know.'

'But I've done nothing wrong. Why should I need protection?'

'You've obviously seen the papers and the photographs. The fact that you were with Kerry Fernandez implies to any other member of the group that you knew more than was good for you.'

'I see,' Sophie muttered. But she didn't see.

'There's a bed upstairs for you. It's made up and, despite the conditions of this place,' she said, indicating the dilapidated surroundings, 'it's clean. I suggest you take forty winks if you can. I've no idea how long we might be here.'

'And what will you do whilst I'm upstairs asleep?'

'I'll sit here and wait. My shift doesn't finish until seven-thirty tomorrow morning. Someone else will come along to relieve me. Go on, love. Give it a try. You'll need to go in for questioning later. We need you to be bright and breezy,' she said, her voice echoing a false laugh.

Sophie went upstairs, took off her trousers and top and climbed into bed. The officer was right. Upstairs was much more welcoming. The sheets and outer covers were clean.

A multitude of thoughts flashed through her mind. It was a good thing her parents knew nothing about this. Her mother would have panicked. She turned and tried to settle herself. They'd had a hectic weekend and in truth Sophie did feel tired. The thoughts became more and more tangled in her mind and unable to make any sense of anything, she must have dropped off to sleep.

It was still dark when she woke up wondering where she was. And then it came to her. She was in that awful house at the other side of the city. Her stomach churned relentlessly. She slipped her legs out of bed and put on her trousers and T-shirt. She could hear voices down below and she stood at the top of the stairs and listened carefully.

'Leave it to me now, Joanne. They've carried out a raid. It's been a success. Nine of them in all including the Fernandez lot. I think Matt's coming along at some point. Seems he has a special interest in the lass upstairs.' He sniggered. 'He knows how to pick 'em, I'll say that for him.'

'When do they want her in for questioning?'

'They don't. They've got all they need. That makes it a bit easier for the boss. He'd have had to back down and let someone else do the questioning. Declare a vested interest, so to speak.'

'I'll leave you to it, Kevin. I'm absolutely whacked. It's a boring job, this, just sitting here waiting.'

'Tell me about it.'

Sophie heard the front door open and close quietly and then she went downstairs. She looked at the clock. It was four thirty.

'Hello there, Miss Jennings. I'm Kevin, replacing Joanne. She's gone off early. How're you feeling?'

'I've slept a little, but I'm worried about Kerry. What'll happen to her?'

'It's too soon to tell, love. The inspector will be in touch as soon as everything is safe.'

It was another two hours before the front door opened and someone stepped inside. Sophie's heart gave a skip. It could be Matt. But she was disappointed. It was another police officer there to take her home to Belmont.

'But I'm quite capable of going home on the train,' she said, a flash of annoyance shimmering through her.

Why was she was being sent home without even seeing Matt? It was obvious he didn't care any longer. She'd been right. He was in Miramar on duty, under-cover, nothing more. Now it all fell into place. He'd taken her out and talked to her in the hope she might tell him about the package. He knew she had it and in desperation in the end he'd been forced to steal it from her room. Being a police officer entailed a little drama, a little acting. That's all it had been an act.

'Sorry we can't let you go alone,' the officer interceded. 'Inspector's instructions. You're to be taken home.'

'If he thinks I'm going to be taken home in a police car like a common criminal, he's another thing coming.' She was outraged. 'And don't I have the courtesy of being told what's happened to my friend Kerry and her family?'

'You won't be calling her your friend when you hear what she's been up to,' the officer replied. The two officers exchanged glances. 'But don't worry, Miss. It won't be a police car. Nobody will know.'

'So you're sending me back without even telling me anything,' she said, having heard part of the story but not telling them that she'd eavesdropped.

'Afraid so, love. You'll find out soon enough, and you'll probably be needed at the trial. But one of your local officers will come and see you about that. They'll explain. Don't worry.'

Sophie picked up her backpack and followed the officers to the door. An unmarked car was parked outside with a plain clothes officer sitting at the wheel. She opened the front passenger door and sat beside him.

'You don't mind if I sit in the front, do you?' she said, knowing full well she'd no intention of sitting in the back. This had to look normal. She didn't want the likes of Mrs Scott or any of her mother's other friends spotting her sitting in the back of a car. That would look suspicious.

The journey was smooth, the officer obviously an experienced driver. Within an hour and a quarter, she was back at her flat. The question now was, should she get ready and go into work, or did she ring in and tell them she wasn't well?

'Enjoy your weekend, Sophie?' It was Val who'd come into the office.

'Wonderful,' Sophie said, making an effort to convey her joy by making sure her blue eyes sparkled. 'We didn't have a minute to spare, meals out, clubbing, shopping,' she added. 'I was absolutely whacked when I got back home last night. Couldn't get into bed quickly enough.'

'Buy anything nice?' Val asked her.

'One or two bits and pieces, but nothing major.'

The telephone rang. Val turned to leave the room. 'Better leave you to get on. I'll see you at lunchtime,' she said.

Sophie picked up the phone. It was Mr Prothero wanting her in X-ray to take notes. She climbed the stairs to his room and sat beside him, taking down his dictation in shorthand but not really thinking about what she was doing. Her mind was on Matt. How could he drag her off to that safe house as though he was worried sick about her and then, when everything was over, ditch her without an explanation.

'Did you get that, Sophie?' Mr Prothero was nudging her on the arm.

'Sorry,' she said,

'I was saying, could you do this one first. I'm seeing the patient this afternoon.'

'Of course,' she said, dragging her mind back to the reports and placing an asterisk next to that particular one. She must concentrate. Although she knew the terminology inside out, she couldn't afford to make any mistakes. As Mr Prothero always said, 'Mistakes can mean lives.'

'I'd like to check what you said there, the last report, if you don't mind. I don't know whether I quite caught it,' she said, knowing she must get it right.

'Sorry, Sophie. I'm not going too fast for you am I?' he asked and then he repeated the words.

'Not at all. All I wanted was to clarify one of the words. I just didn't catch it clearly.'

Afterwards she left the room and

went back downstairs, telling herself she must get on with the reports and keep her mind on them too. No more thinking about Matt or any of that police business.

She rattled them off quickly, checked through them and printed them off ready for Mr Prothero. She took them back upstairs to his office.

'There, I've finished the lot. The one you wanted urgently is on top.'

'Well done, Sophie. The orthopaedic surgeon will be here shortly. We need to discuss the case before the patient arrives.'

Sophie returned to her office and, after that, the day seemed to drag. Although she'd missed the Friday, for some unknown reason there was virtually no backlog. It would probably all fall on her desk tomorrow. She couldn't sit there twiddling her thumbs. The filing cabinet needed a good sort out to make sure the patient records were in the correct order. Sometimes when she was in a rush, she slipped them back into the cabinet at the front to file later.

Hauling out an armful, she started to sort them. But her mind was buzzing again. What would happen to Kerry? Sophie assumed she'd be given some sort of sentence just like the rest. But what had they done? Surely someone could have given her some inkling as to what was going on.

She desperately needed to tell someone what had happened and to talk it through with them. It was on the tip of her tongue to confide in Val when they sat and ate lunch together. But Sophie knew it would be wrong to divulge anything, especially when she'd not been told the full story herself. They talked about the weekend and of meeting up with Justin, but Sophie didn't mention anything about Matt, not even the fact that she'd been given his address and telephone number.

In any case, phoning Matt was out of the question now. She wouldn't dream of it, not after what had happened. He hadn't had the courtesy to contact her. A phone call at the safe house would have sufficed. He could have intimated he needed to know something.

The officers didn't have to know what it was all about. But that triggered in her mind the comment made by one of them about his having some interest in her. How did they make that out? Had he said something or was it just their interpretation of things?

After lunch, Sophie continued to sort out the filing cabinet, but then she was called upstairs to the operating theatre by Mr Richards.

'I've one or two notes I need you to take down, Sophie, the two ops I've completed this afternoon. You have the records of these two I take it,' he asked, pointing to the names on his list.

'Yes. They're in the cabinet,' she replied as she opened her notebook and started to take down his dictation.

Back down in her office she sat at the computer, referring to the notes on her desk and opening the appropriate records. She concentrated on the notes Mr Richards had dictated, hoping she could complete them before the end of the afternoon. She didn't quite manage it by five o'clock and she decided to stay over and complete them.

'Doing a spot of overtime?' Val asked, slipping on her coat ready to set off for the bus.

'I've nothing to rush back for, Val. I thought I might finish these before I leave.'

'See you tomorrow, love,' Val called out and she set out up the drive. But within minutes she was back again. She opened the door to Sophie's office, popped her head round it and smiled. 'There's someone outside waiting for you.'

'Who is it?' Sophie asked casually, still continuing to process the reports.

'He didn't say but he's rather a hunk, dark hair, gorgeous brown eyes.'

Startled, Sophie looked up. Dark hair and gorgeous brown eyes! It couldn't be!

'I'll be out in a minute, Val,' she said trying not to show her delight.

'It's him, isn't it, Soph?'

Sophie nodded.

'Good luck. Tell me all about it tomorrow. I must go. Don't want to miss my bus.' She dashed out of the door and Sophie watched her putting on an extra spurt as she went up the drive and out towards the main road.

She switched off the computer and collected her things. She was shaking now as she left the building and made for the car park.

Her heart did a double-take. He was there, leaning on her car, that familiar sparkle lighting up his eyes. Sophie looked deep into them and a smile trembled on her lips.

'You're not getting rid of me that easily,' he said, taking her hands in his and pulling her towards him.

'What are you doing here, Matt? It's a long way from home,' she said, determined not to give in too easily.

'I owe you an explanation, darling.

Come with me. My car's over there.'

He'd touched a nerve. 'Here we go again. It seems you give the orders and I toe the line, come running,' she said, shaking her head. 'But not any more Inspector Williams.' She waved her hand dismissively.

'We'll see about that,' he said, grinning and pulling her closer. 'Are you going to do as I ask, or do I have to take you by force?'

Her body froze. She wanted desperately to stay close to him. But somehow she couldn't let herself. 'No, Matt. There are things I have to say to you first.'

'Fire away, darling,' he said, still holding her firm against his body. 'But we had a genuine case to deal with. I didn't intend acting so coldly towards you. But at that moment in time, there was nothing more I could do. I needed you out of harm's way. Don't you understand? Any one of them could have taken you hostage.'

Her eyes widened. 'So it was that serious.'

'It most certainly was. Come along now, Soph. What was it you had to say?'

'It's not important.' She felt deflated. There she was ready to climb on to her high horse again and all he'd wanted was to protect her.

'Then, let's get away and I can explain it all to you. How about if I come back with you to your place?'

Wow. She'd like him to come back with her, but could she trust herself? The answer was yes. She'd proved to herself she could be strong. There was no reason why she could change all of a sudden.

'I've got to admit I was disappointed not to be told what was happening. I do need an explanation, Matt. But if you don't mind, I'll take my own car back to the flat. You can follow me. If anyone comes around to the flat, I don't want them to think I haven't arrived home.'

'No monkey business. Go straight home, promise me.' He squeezed her hands and kissed her lightly on the cheek.

'Promise,' she said and her heart began to beat louder than ever in her chest. He had a lot of explaining to do. But she'd listen. He deserved that at least.

She slid the key in the lock and opened the door to the flat, closing it quietly behind them. She was about to walk through into the lounge when he took hold of her shoulders and pressed her against the door, placing his lips on hers and letting them stay there for a long, lingering moment. Her heart skipped. That was round one she'd lost.

He let her go and whispered, 'I had to do that, darling,' his eyes smiling lovingly into hers. 'Now I can proceed,' he added with a certain formality. He led her through into the lounge and they sat down.

'I was out in Spain to chase up information on a massive smuggling ring, a combined group, Spaniards and Brits. They start out by stealing exotic jewellery from some of the Asian countries and smuggling it back into the country. Customs and Excise have been on to them for some time, the smuggling side that is.

'Our task has been to liaise with the police in Saudi and Kuwait, and then to follow certain leads.' He slipped his hand into his pocket and brought out a small brown envelope.

'Your friend and mine, Kerry, has been working incognito as a wealthy Muslim woman interested in buying expensive jewellery. And believe it or not, she is a very experienced shoplifter. The photographs you had were passed on to me by the Saudi police.' He opened the envelope and brought out the photographs, the ones from the package.

'These were taken on video in a shop she visited with her father,' he said waving them in the air. 'Somehow, one of their gang stole my briefcase and, to get rid of the package quickly, instead of passing it on to Kerry by hand, they slipped it into what they thought was her suitcase. She was supposed to check out the contents, the lists and things, and later dispose of them.'

'That figures,' Sophie said. 'I never saw Kerry's suitcase. She left early on our departure day. The only person I knew with a suitcase similar to mine was you. I must confess, at one point I honestly thought the package belonged to you.'

'I realised that, once I knew you had it, but I couldn't give you an explanation. We were too close to finding out the truth at that point.'

'So you knew right from the start I had the package.'

'Not immediately. I checked out Kerry's stuff first and then, of course, I had all the others to check before I finally came to yours.'

'I don't know about Kerry being an experienced shoplifter, you must be an experienced cat burglar.' She laughed. 'I was amazed when the package disappeared.'

'I knew you would be.'

'Why didn't the thief destroy the

package once he'd retrieved it from your briefcase?'

'They needed the sheets with the indexing for their own purposes. And they needed to destroy the photographs which were solid evidence. You see they had been passed on by an accomplice who worked at the shop where some of the jewellery was stolen. But things obviously happened so quickly, there wasn't time. And, believe it or not, although the two people on the photographs couldn't be identified at first, we now know they were Kerry and her father.'

'Kerry and her father. I would never have thought it when I looked at the photographs. But I suppose with her deep Mediterranean complexion Kerry could easily pass herself off as an Asian woman in the typical purdah clothing. No-one would suspect.'

'Exactly. But that's not the end of the story. You remember the fight in the club on the playa?'

'I do, most vividly.'

'They were two of the gang members. They'd obviously had a few drinks and one of them started to argue — something to do with money I suspect. If you remember, Kerry said when she read the newspaper there was probably some connection with football gangs. That was to throw us off the scent. But she didn't fool me.'

'I'm absolutely amazed, darling, that Kerry was involved. I would never have suspected it.'

'Did I hear you right? You did call me darling, didn't you?'

She nodded and before she could say any more, his lips planted themselves over hers, silencing her. She closed her eyes tightly and wrapped her arms gently around his neck. The kiss was soft at first and then it became more urgent, making up for the weeks of abstinence. And then he eased away from her and smiled.

Her eyes widened and she returned his smile. There was no need for them to speak. Sophie snuggled into his shoulder. At that moment they knew exactly what was going through each other's minds, what was happening to each other's hearts.

After a long silence, she whispered, 'Yes, I did call you darling,' and he responded with a look that confirmed all she needed to know.

THE END

We do hope that you have enjoyed reading this large print book.

Did you know that all of our titles are available for purchase?

We publish a wide range of high quality large print books including:
Romances, Mysteries, Classics
General Fiction
Non Fiction and Westerns

Special interest titles available in large print are:
The Little Oxford Dictionary
Music Book, Song Book
Hymn Book, Service Book

Also available from us courtesy of Oxford University Press:
Young Readers' Dictionary
(large print edition)
Young Readers' Thesaurus
(large print edition)

For further information or a free brochure, please contact us at:
Ulverscroft Large Print Books Ltd.,
The Green, Bradgate Road, Anstey,
Leicester, LE7 7FU, England.
Tel: (00 44) **0116 236 4325**
Fax: (00 44) **0116 234 0205**

Other titles in the
Linford Romance Library:

HER HEART'S DESIRE

Dorothy Taylor

When Beth Garland's great aunt Emily dies, she leaves Greg, her boyfriend, in Manchester — along with her successful advertising job — to return to live in Emily's cottage. Feeling disillusioned with Greg and his high-handed attitude, she finds herself more and more attracted to her aunt's gardener, Noah. But Noah seems to be hiding from the past, whilst Greg has his own ideas about the direction of their relationship. Surrounded by secrecy and deceit, how will Beth ever find true love?

PRECIOUS MOMENTS

June Gadsby

The heartbreak was all behind her, but hearing her name mentioned on the radio, and that song — their special song — brought bittersweet memories rushing back through the years. It had to be a coincidence, and was best forgotten — but then Lara opened the door to find her past standing there. The moment of truth she had dreaded for years had finally arrived, and she wasn't sure how to handle it . . .